AF447519

# TWISTED GENOME

## A novel by
## F.L. BARSTOW III

Twisted Genome is a work of fiction. Names, characters, businesses, organizations, places, events, and incidents are the product of the author's imagination, or are used fictitiously. Any resemblance to actual persons, living, dead, or locales is entirely coincidental.

This book is dedicated to

*Mary Barstow*

# CHAPTER 1

# It Can Be a Slippery Slope

Ten years of work were now ready to be tested. Dr. Zeke Leonard carefully placed the fertilized embryo and DNA sample from a neighbor's dog in the Biotech sequencing machine that he had been painstakingly building over these years.

His patience through the many low times of trial and error and failure had gradually been rewarded with small steps forward. It was sweet vindication. Over a decade ago, after working for Waltham Scientific Bioworks in Waltham, Massachusetts for nearly ten years, Dr. Leonard had been unceremoniously dismissed. He had been directing his team on a valuable project—one that Zeke saw as having tremendous global potential in addressing food shortages. But the Waltham Scientific Bioworks Board of Directors had disagreed with his work, and after some heated discussions, Zeke was summarily let go—cast out. The project stopped in its tracks.

He had therefore been relieved and surprised that, within a month of his dismissal, he found funding for his project. His benefactor, whose identity was still a mystery to him, had reached out to him and simply asked him, through anonymous contacts, how much money he needed to continue his work. Dr. Leonard had discussed this generous offer with his wife Jane, as he did with most important matters. Jane was impressed with Zeke's desire to help the world's food supply and believed in his work. But some aspects of what he was doing made her uneasy, since it involved developing sophisticated cloning capabilities. She had wondered if Zeke had considered all aspects of the research and knew what he was getting in for. But Zeke had convinced her he would put in place whatever ethical and legal safeguards were necessary as his project developed. They agreed that the anonymous donor's offer was perfect for a research scientist. Large sums of money, no strings, no interference, and only minimal quarterly reports expected, by way of monitoring. Zeke agreed to the terms and took the money. As his work progressed over the past ten years, he had requested over fifteen million in funding. He always got the requested funds the next day in his company's bank account. He provided the routine quarterly reports on his progress and continued his work without comments, critiques, or suggestions from the benefactor. Now, finally, he felt this next test could bring this phase of his work to a successful close.

Zeke was now fifty years old. As a child he had been recognized as a genius with extraordinary aptitude in science. By the time he was seven, he was taking science courses at a local community college. By the time he was twelve, he was accepted at Harvard, and his family moved to Boston from his Southern California home. At eighteen, he was hired by a Cambridge biotech company. At thirty, he moved to Waltham Scientific Bioworks. During the next five years, his team produced some notable, ambitious advancements in the biomedical field. These discoveries made Zeke both known and respected among his colleagues. He approached every subject as a scientist, in a methodical, reasonable, and questioning way. People said fondly of him, "You can tell he is a scientist in the first five minutes you talk to him, even if you are not talking about science." While with Waltham Scientific he travelled to Europe, Asia, Africa, and South America, working with scientists in other countries and presenting papers to the scientific community, on the discoveries he and his team had established. Wherever he went, he tried to see the notable landmarks and wonders of the world, knowing that much of his working life was lived in labs.

A tall man with dark brown hair and a mustache, Zeke was about 6 feet 4 inches tall and weighed a trim 190 pounds. He stood out at conferences and in his lab, with a commanding presence and a friendly, benevolent air. His countenance was usually serious, but he also found it easy to laugh at himself. He was serious, that is, but he didn't take himself too seriously. People thought of him as a kind and caring man, observant of others' feelings and needs. He was known as someone who could always be depended upon.

Zeke had gotten married at thirty-one to Jane Seymour, a molecular scientist herself, deeply involved in the aging process and how to slow it down. In contrast to the impression that Zeke made, her community of friends did not think she had the appearance of a scientist. She was about 5 feet 4 inches tall, blonde, with a classic hourglass figure. Jane was outgoing—a fun person to be around. She had a natural charm and a cheerful disposition. When she and Zeke met at a science conference in San Francisco, it was love at first sight, on both sides. Over the years they had developed a language of their own that they used with each other. It was so technical that it made them laugh. Almost every day after work, they would sit in the study of their modest home in Nashua, New Hampshire, and talk about the projects that they were working on, the progress made, or problems encountered. In the study, the couple would unwind and share their respective scientific lives--Jane speaking of her work at the biomedical lab, and Zeke of his experiments. As they threw their ideas back and forth, their voices would rise in excitement. They would trade quips and comments about how to build a better this or a better that in the lab. At times they would get so excited about their conversation they would end up making out and would end up in bed. They would continue sharing ideas about their lab work right up to an exhausted, talkative end of their love making.

They had discussed having children and rather quickly chose not to because a family would interfere with their work. As they went through their thirties and then their forties, however, Zeke had started to regret that decision. Both of Zeke's parents had passed away in their early seventies when Zeke was in his mid-forties. Jane was an only child, and her parents were now in their late seventies. He worried that someday in the future, when one of them was gone, the other would be left without close family in this world, and that thought would depress him. It would grab hold of his soul and give him a heavy heart and a sense of unease. He loved Jane so much he never wanted her to be alone. He never talked to her about this matter, but she could see something was wrong. When he went into these funks, she wondered what was bothering him. She would give him space and time until he would emerge himself again, sometimes in a few hours, sometimes days later.

It was during one of these spells of depression that Zeke suddenly turned to Jane and said, "Let's go to Puerto Rico for a quick vacation. I really feel like I need a break. I know things are kind of crazy in the country right now with this new president and all these strikes and marches, but let us escape."

"You will never hear me say no to a trip to Old San Juan," Jane answered. "Great country, great people. Yes, let's go for it!

I'll call work in the morning on the way to the airport. My schedule is clear."

Jane and Zeke took off the next morning. As they got off the plane in Puerto Rico, the beautiful warm weather of September embraced them. They headed over to the Hilton Hotel, holding each other's hand as if they were teenagers in a new relationship. They simply liked each other so much that they expressed affection easily and naturally. Their deep love for each other followed.

After checking in, Zeke said, "Let's find our room upstairs, get into swimsuits, and hit the beach. It is a beautiful day. I want to read for a while on a chaise, order some lunch, and just chill."

"Okay. Sounds good. Maybe a little late afternoon nap, too," Jane said to him. They both needed this break. Though they were highly committed professionals who loved their work, it wore on them sometimes. They both had their heads in their own "scientific clouds," and when Zeke had been let go, many years ago now, it had been heartbreaking to both of them. They shared so much of their work with each other that they had both felt fired. At the time, Jane could not believe Waltham Scientific had not seen the benefit of Zeke's ideas. Gradually, she herself had started to question the efficacy of Zeke's work. Would it work? And if it did, could the powerful forces it unleashed be controlled? She had expressed this to Zeke, she was concerned. In any event, they had long ago both accepted his termination and moved on, feeling with hindsight that perhaps it was even for the best. The generous funding of the anonymous donor had softened the sting of Waltham Scientific's rejection. Now they just worked long hours, looking neither to right nor left, until they took a break like this one.

They had noticed that the resort was not crowded, as it had been on other visits. That evening they went to the hotel restaurant, and they did not have to wait to be seated. It had been about a year and a half ago since they had been here, so they were surprised and pleased that the maître d' remembered them by name.

"Dr. Leonard and Dr. Jane, how wonderful to have you back at our establishment. Welcome," Carlos said with a bow.

"Carlos, nice to see you again. Good to be back. Tell me, is Caesar salad still a specialty of the house?" Jane asked.

"Yes, we'll make you two of the best Caesar salads in the hemisphere. As I remember it, Dr. Leonard, you like a good number of anchovies."

"You've got that right, Carlos. And that is a surprisingly good memory, my friend. Carlos, let me ask you a question. This place is empty, the beaches are empty, what's going on?" Zeke asked.

"Well, if I can speak freely, it is the new policies that President Bartlett has put in place, affecting the Island," he answered. "His measures have killed tourism. So many people have lost their jobs that there is no money to visit here. It has been getting worse by the month."

Zeke, always absorbed in his work, had read only a little about these matters. He had been aware there were problems with this new President, but not that unemployment and the economy had worsened to this extent. Jane was more attuned to these political and social problems, but in her and Zeke's relationship if it wasn't about science, they didn't talk about it.

Over dinner, Jane wanted to talk about some family business, about Zeke's recent lab work. She had been concerned for some time as to where his research was going. She knew that Zeke's theory was that he could produce a genetically controlled calf or sheep in a day, using an artificial womb or cloning chamber that dramatically shortened the animal's normal gestation time. He envisioned hundreds of these chambers creating a vast supply of these animals, these clones, at an accelerated rate, to address global food shortages. He felt that this breakthrough could help countries around the world where people did not have enough to eat. Zeke's old company had disagreed. The people in charge had feared that the world would see Waltham Scientific not as solving the problem of famine but as creating the technology for made-to-order test-tube human babies produced outside the womb. In their view, what Zeke was developing would lead inevitably to human clones, genetically programmed to be whatever way a client wanted. Zeke never saw that scenario as an option or as even technically feasible. But if Zeke were successful with animals, Waltham Scientific was concerned that unscrupulous people would step in and abuse this technology. They wanted no part of this research.

Now, Jane was getting concerned, too. She realized that, much as she respected and admired Zeke, she had always doubted that his work would ever come to fruition. Yes, he might create an artificial womb. Maybe, and that was a big maybe, he could accelerate the gestation period. That was doubtful. But tonight, she felt compelled to warn him that if any of these breakthroughs came to pass, he—they—could be in for a lot of trouble and bad publicity. Zeke said again that he believed he could make these advancements happen and that they would be a "net positive" for the world. And that he felt he was getting close—that was what excited him. Little did he know that as he got closer to a solution, he was getting closer to going in a direction he never, ever imagined and changes in the world he could never have anticipated.

"For now," he pleaded, "let's forget about the world and just be the two of us in this universe. After dinner, we will go for a walk on the beach and find a spot to stare at the moon over the ocean together."

Jane conceded the point and let go of the subject. Work and the troubling questions that surrounded it could wait. Zeke was such a nerd when he tried to be romantic, but she loved it. "Sounds perfect," she said, "and later maybe we can watch a movie."

After five days of lounging, swimming, sipping piña coladas, and drifting to their room for afternoon naps and some afternoon delights, they both were ready to get back. The refocus on each other, in a place of azure water and pink beaches, had been just what their bodies and souls needed. Now, they felt the call of pressing duties. So, the following Sunday they were off. They were returning to a world which would never be the same.

# CHAPTER 2

# Eureka!

"Martha, set the Wilcott sequencing machine in a position where I can activate it when necessary," Zeke said to his assistant.

"Do you want me to start the gene spinney thing too?" Martha was a good assistant for Zeke. She was very bright and of real help, but she tended to not be so technical in her language when referring to work they did in Zeke's lab. Martha had created words and terms that they both used to communicate—their own language of the lab. And her lack of technical vocabulary was okay from Zeke's view because he did not want an assistant who knew exactly what he was working on. She accepted this limitation willingly.

Martha had arrived at his heavy green steel lab door unexpectedly when he first started assembling his equipment ten years ago. He had not yet advertised for an assistant, so he was surprised when she appeared one day. Her resume was surprisingly strong. She had graduated from Columbia with honors and had spent twenty years with the CDC. Her last ten years were simply stated as being in private employ conducting research. Little detail, but Zeke hired her, and the arrangement had worked out well for both of them. Now fifty-five, she was semi-retired. They were both around the same age, and they were comfortable around each other. Zeke would sometimes muse on how he found Martha so accidently, or rather how she had found him.

"Yes, accelerate the genes in the spinny thing on my command," Zeke said, instead of saying, "Start the gene CRISPR." Suddenly the laboratory was alive with a low humming noise that gradually increased, as Zeke engaged the Wilcott equipment that had taken him years to modify and perfect for his purposes. Zeke had the traditional CRISPR equipment to get the DNA he wanted out of a cell and insert the DNA sequencing he desired. He had a storage area where he kept his fertilized samples in a deep freeze alphabetized by species, including himself under "Homo Sapiens." Why he did that he never could figure out, but he did. Automatically his equipment would insert the fertilized embryo with his chosen DNA.

A Dr. Wilcott had developed a CRISPR years ago to create genes to fight illness or infection. Zeke had acquired this equipment and modified it over several painstaking years to be able to sequence up to three billion pairs at a time of the A, C, T and G codes that can be strung together to make biological instructions that govern cells. The laboratory he created was located on the industrial side of town among dozens of warehouses. It had a brick exterior with opaque windows that were twelve feet up from the ground. The windows let in light, but no one could see in, even if they could reach them. Ivy was growing on some areas of the exterior. There was a large green steel door that led directly into the lab area, with no reception room. The lab was where fertilized embryos and DNA were stored and all his equipment--lab tables, microscopes, and a myriad of other equipment either purchased or built by Zeke over the past ten years.

As Zeke engaged other equipment in a sequence, he had perfected it, it started to draw on the electricity, dimming the lights in the lab. Now the humming had reached its peak, and Zeke and Martha had to raise their voices slightly to be heard. "Insert the DNA samples and the embryo into the birthing chamber," Zeke bellowed. Martha carefully inserted the samples in a clear glass container in a slot that was pushed into the birthing chamber. At this point Zeke turned to Martha and said she could leave for the day. She was not surprised by this order, as whenever they got to this point in the experiment, she was asked to leave. She was prepared. Her sweater and purse lay on a chair next to her, a chair that she had brought to the lab just for this purpose.

"Take care, Doctor. I hope whatever you want to happen happens this time."

"Thanks, Martha. Me, too." His goals were left that vague.

Zeke stared into the birthing chamber where the DNA sample and fertilized embryo was located. For the next ninety minutes Zeke did not move from his equipment, always checking gauges and the pressure inside the "birthing chamber." He thought about all the other experiments and the results that he had gotten. The last had been the most promising. He had been shocked when he opened the birthing chamber and what emerged was not a newborn pup but a fully mature dog. It was a two-year-old German shepherd, awake, alert, and friendly, and identical to his neighbor's dog whose DNA he had used. Zeke checked his records. The fertilized dog embryo had been in the birthing chamber for twelve hours, four minutes, and seventeen seconds. All his calculations showed the result would be a newborn puppy. Instead, everything about the dog was full-grown and perfect. Zeke had created a clone that was born mature, a dog that played catch, ate food, and drank water. Zeke took the new dog out for a walk and let it do its business. He kept the dog a secret, keeping it in the lab and keeping Martha away. All seemed well for forty-seven days. Then suddenly the dog had sickened. Its torso started to droop dramatically. Its eyes aged quickly and almost fell out of its head. Suddenly the aging process of the dog accelerated by years every minute that ticked by and within twenty minutes of Zeke noticing a change the dog had died. It was as if the skeletal part of the dog had matured properly, but the organs had not. So, Zeke had spent nearly a year checking and rechecking his data, adjusting. His work was breaking into areas he had never envisioned. He thought now he may have it all sequenced in a way where he could plan to create a mature dog . . . this time on purpose. His dream now was creating mature herds of animals, quickly solving the world's hunger issues and saving the environment. This unexpected development was better than he had ever imagined.

The equipment in Zeke's laboratory continued operating for two full days—for forty-eight hours and fifty-three minutes to be exact. In all his other efforts he had run the process from as little as two hours to as much as twelve hours. After dissecting the remains of the dog he had created, he saw that it was a fully mature animal, but there was no question the animal's organs had skipped the maturing process. So, the animal's aging process began to accelerate, and what he saw was the dog suddenly growing older by the second and then dying. Zeke had reviewed the entire process, the films he made of the dog, the physical readings he took continuously of the dog.

He was certain he knew what was wrong. Even though the dog appeared to be and acted like a mature animal, internally not enough time had been allocated in the birthing room for the animal's systems to stabilize.

What fascinated him about the dog was that it seemed to "know" how to act as a mature dog. He knew the people who had the original dog and knew that it was trained. While Zeke had him, he tested him on all the commands the owners had told him they had taught the dog, and sure enough the dog responded. So, it became apparent that the DNA sample was helping to create a dog at some point in its life. At the end of the day of working continuously on his calculations and watching his equipment operate, he went home for the first time in over eighteen hours. As he approached the house, he noticed that all the lights were off. The street Zeke and Jane lived on was the quintessential tree-lined neighborhood. It was a quiet and a safe place to live.

The shrubbery in front of the house was overgrown, and Zeke made a mental note that, as soon as he could, he would trim them back a little.

He opened the door and yelled out, "Jane, I'm home." His doing that always made him think of the old films he saw of "Leave it to Beaver" and how the Beavs's father would call out, "June, I home."

"I'm here," Jane replied. "In the study." She was sitting on the sofa, sipping a perfect Manhattan. That was her favorite alcoholic drink, and she knew how to make it just sweet enough, leaving out the slice of lemon and adding a cherry. Technically, it was not correct for a perfect Manhattan to have a cherry in it, but it was just the way she liked it.

"Is your experiment finished already? I thought you were going to run it two full days." "I'm home for a break to see you," Zeke said, as he put his arms around her and gave her a kiss.

"Well, aren't you sweet? Would you like a taste?" Zeke was not much of a drinker, but he would occasionally stop at a local pub on the way home from the lab and have a drink or one at home with his wife.

"No, I'll get some iced tea and join you," Zeke said. Zeke could see that Jane had already eaten supper, but there were some meatballs and spaghetti left. He scooped up a healthy serving and put it in the microwave. Cook it just long enough, he thought— not too little or too much. Pretty much the same sweet spot he was trying to find in the lab.

"You know," Zeke said as he entered the study and sat down, "This spaghetti hits the spot. Is this your mother's recipe for the sauce?"

"No. I did talk to her today, but it is all mine, dear. I added several diced carrots to sweeten it up. I wanted it to match the sweetness of my perfect Manhattan," Jane said, smiling. She could see that Zeke had been up for most of the day and a half he had been gone. She worried about him at times like this, when he was so absorbed in applying his theory he forgot to eat.

She looked around this familiar room, the scene of so many conversations between them. Here they had speculated on the identity of Zeke's secret benefactor, this person who was still financing his efforts so freely and requiring only quarterly reports on his progress. Who would do that and why? It must be a philanthropist, someone who shares Zeke's vision of helping the world's food supply. In this room they had discussed the efficacy of these experiments. Today Jane was ready with new information that she had gleaned from some notes Zeke had brought home earlier in the week.

"Zeke, I read some of your notes yesterday. I am not sure I understand what they mean. You were talking about a test-tube animal you had created. A clone. That I get. But it is this part I don't understand—that it lived and died of old age? What do you mean? A fertilized embryo was born years ago and failed to survive a normal life? I am confused."

Hearing the critical tone underneath her questions, Zeke tried to find the best words to respond. He decided on an honest, straightforward approach, since he saw nothing wrong with what he was doing. "As you know, I have created an artificial womb, so my clones don't need a natural womb to develop in. And I wanted to accelerate the maturation time so these cloned animals could be produced at a rapid rate as newborn calves, sheep, etc. But surprise, surprise, a dog I was cloning was born as a mature dog inside of my birthing chamber, not as a newborn pup as I had expected. I kept him in the lab for over a month. I did not mention him to you as I wanted to wait and see what would happen to him, and I wanted to try and figure out how the heck this happened. Amazingly I was able to produce a mature cloned dog in this chamber after the embryo with the DNA was in there for only twelve hours."

Jane sat up straight and stared at Zeke. Her mouth was slightly agape, and her drink frozen in her hand. No one said anything for a full minute.

Jane was stunned. "Are you telling me you are creating a clone of an animal outside of a natural womb, and you have learned how to manipulate the fertilized embryo and DNA into a mature animal? That is impossible, Zeke."

"I've been getting closer to achieving this over the past eighteen months. Jane, think of this. Can you imagine making my birthing chamber available to a country of people who are undernourished? With a hundred pieces of my equipment set up in labs around the world, I could create a herd of mature cows, sheep, and pigs in a day. In a week, I could create tens of thousands of animals. Herds. And they would be no burden on the environment"

"You need to stop this whole thing right now," Jane said in an intense tone. This new vision he had just sketched out had completely unnerved her. While she had stated having reservations years ago, this new revelation sent her over the edge. How could he not see this as a problem? How had she let this go as far as it did? How had he? It was a big mistake. Never would she support this new goal. He was playing God. She now agreed with the Board of Directors at Waltham Scientific Bioworks and could see with new clarity why they had wanted no part of Zeke's work. If they ever knew that, besides accelerating the maturation time of a clone's development, he could also create a mature animal they would have tried to bar him from the scientific community globally. They feared, as Jane did now, that somewhere, someone would pervert this technological advancement and figure out how to clone people. Before you would know it, grieving parents would want to use the DNA from a six-year-old child who had just died from an accident, and in a day have him or her back, good as new.

The invention opened a brave new world beyond anyone's understanding, desire, or acceptance.

"Zeke, you need to stop," Jane said. "What you are doing will wreak havoc on our lives and maybe on the whole world. The delicate balance between life and death will be destroyed. You must stop." Jane was in a panic now, agitated in a way that Zeke had never seen her. Zeke looked wide-eyed at her.

"Don't you see how the process you have developed can be abused?" Jane kept on. "Soon it will go from animals being born mature, to babies made to order, or people who want to keep cloning their younger selves and live forever. As one copy dies out it would then be replaced with another. Eventually, everyone would be clamoring for immortality. That is what you have created here: immortality."

"That is not my intent, Jane, and you know it. That idea is ridiculous. I would never even try to clone a person. Never. My idea is to help the world's food supply—that is all. Creating a "made-to-order" person was never, is never, going to be a part of this invention. I cannot stop now, Jane. Do I know . . . the secret of creation? No, I can't say that, but I know the secret to . . . to. . . .." His voice trailed off with each word he spoke. What secret had he unearthed? He had opened a Pandora's Box. Had he crossed the line? It was now frightening them both.

"No, you must stop. Stop, stop, stop. You are too good and naïve to see this, but you cannot go forward with these experiments. They need to be shut down and shut down forever" Jane was in an absolute panic. The color had earlier drained from her face, but now she turned red with anger and agitation. Zeke sat up, frightened at her intensity.

"What you are doing is against nature and against all we know that is holy and ethical," she begged. "Potentially creating a human baby outside the womb, a clone, is diabolical enough and is one abomination but, picking its age, this is *crazy*! You cannot do this! Look, Zeke, you have to see how this invention could potentially be abused. I know you think only of positive outcomes and advancements for the good for the world, but there are bad people out there, Zeke. They could take terrible advantage of this."

"Jane, I would never let that happen. I would never even do an experiment with that in mind. I would create roadblocks to allow that from happening. I would think of something to make sure that never, ever happened." Zeke was begging his wife to understand. "Oh, my chest, I feel faint. Zeke, help me."

Jane suddenly grabbed at her head. And then it happened. Jane fell over on her face, landing hard. Her drink fell, smashing on the tile. She was dying before Zeke's eyes as she fell forward to the floor. Zeke rushed to her side. He felt the pulse. Nothing. He turned Jane over and started pumping on her chest. But he knew. He could tell. He snatched her phone and punched in her code and called 911.

"What is your emergency?" asked the dispatcher. "It's my wife! She has had a stroke or heart attack! Hurry, please!" He gave their address on Reed Street.

"Does she have a pulse and is she breathing? Do you have any aspirin to administer to your wife?"

That question from the 911 operator was the last thing that he remembered. He was a scientist. He understood life and death better than most. He knew he had just lost the love of his life, in the heat of a terrible argument. It was too much for his brain to handle. He went into shock. When he came to, he was in an ambulance next to his wife, who was dead.

**CHAPTER 3**

# The Awakening

The funeral was almost more that Zeke could bear. Jane's parents were there, along with hundreds of friends, colleagues, and acquaintances. The house was jammed with people, many talking about Jane, remembering the kind, brilliant scientist she was.

"I am just lost, lost," Zeke whispered to Jane's mother and father.

"We all are," Jane's mother responded. "There is now a hole in all our lives that will always be there." "I should have been able to save her," Zeke said, irrationally. Zeke had asked for an autopsy, and the medical examiner had confirmed that Jane's left anterior descending artery, leading to the heart, was 99 percent clogged. No one could have saved her. But with her dying in the middle of such an intense discussion, Zeke still could not help but blame himself. He had thought she might have had a stroke, brought on by the sudden stress of their argument. No, the report established that she had a time bomb in her chest, ready to explode, probably for more than a year. Unless she had discovered her condition earlier, in the course of a medical checkup, or had gotten some other signs, it was going to happen.

After three painful hours everyone had departed. Some of Jane's closest friends lingered behind to assure Zeke they were there for him if he needed anything. Zeke thanked them all and finally, finally bid them goodbye. He sat and stared outside for a long time. Then he decided to get up and go to the lab, his place of refuge. What else was he going to do?

Zeke opened the big green steel door of his lab and switched on the lights. When Martha heard about Jane's passing, she had gone to the lab to make sure everything was okay. She knew Zeke had been in the middle of another experiment. She had shut all the equipment down. Now he was entering the lab for the first time in almost ten days. The sight of his lab helped settle his mind. Before he had left, he had started another experiment on the DNA he had received from a local source that usually manufacturers synthetic DNA to order. Zeke went to his bench and looked over his notes.

With Jane gone, Zeke sensed that he was losing his bearings. To cope, he was mentally in another world. He was blocking out as much emotion as he could. He thought endlessly about their last confrontation. Should he just stop all his research and experimentation, or was Jane wrong? In his mind it was an unfinished discussion. If he had had more time, he would have convinced her. He kept clinging to the thought that Jane did not fully understand what he was trying to do. He could implement safeguards. He could patent his process and keep it secret for at least seventeen years. He was a scientist, and as a scientist he had to play out this effort until his theory was either completely proven or proved to be impossible. He decided he had to continue, to see what he had started to its logical conclusion. If after he proved to himself that he could do what he thought he could do, if it seemed immoral or wrong or he couldn't protect it from being abused, he would destroy his notes and shut down the lab. But not until then. He had to find out. He was sure he knew why the dog had aged so quickly. He knew the answer was right in front of him. He found that focusing on his work helped him deal with the pain of Jane being gone. The ache in his chest subsided as he got lost in the formulas and calculations he was reviewing.

He stayed at this work for the next twelve hours, finally falling asleep in the chair that was placed in the corner of the lab. It was the one Martha used when she got tired and where she put her sweater, shawl, or jacket. He awoke a few hours later, stretched, and went back to work.

On Wednesday morning, October 27, three weeks after the funeral, Zeke was reviewing some areas of his calculations where he felt he had made the longevity error of his test subject. Zeke spent a long time studying genetic mutations, first studied years ago by the Salk Institute for Biological Studies. Jane had been immensely helpful in sharing the work in this area with him. Her laboratory had been able to manipulate some genetic codes which reversed aging. They had not been able to stop the mutation, and the subject mice would die of "young age." Organs would fail or form tumors as a result of the genetic manipulation. Before Jane died, she had shared in minute detail how her lab felt they could control this mutation in the future. With Jane's notes, he thought he might find a way to at least control the rapid deterioration of his cloned animal. Later that afternoon, with Martha dutifully reviewing all the equipment, they were ready to try again. This would be the 859th experiment, covering much more time than seven days God needed to create the universe and man. As the equipment started to accelerate, Martha grabbed her light fall coat from the chair and headed for the door.

Zeke stood to let her out. As a scientist, he had to follow his work to the logical end. He had to. He thought again, Jane was wrong. He could help the world. He knew he could. He would finish this test and then he would decide what to do with it.

"Are you sure you are up to this, Doctor? You have been through so much, and you haven't taken a second for yourself," Martha said, gently touching his arm.

"Martha, this experiment is the only thing that is saving my sanity. For now, I need a distraction. The pain is so difficult. I hope you understand. I am going to take a break after this experiment is finished. So, wait for my call before coming back. It could be a while."

Martha responded, "Sure, Doctor." But she was surprised since he had never talked of an extended break before. As she left, they both wondered if they would ever work together again, or if she was leaving the lab for the last time. This experiment could be the culmination of over ten years of working together. Oh, how wrong they were. It was going to take a while for these billions of genes to receive their instructions to reconstruct an animal. Zeke had modified his equipment, based upon Jane's notes, to reprogram his subject animal and to reset the body's epigenetic marks. This adjusted equipment was now in sync for the first time.

Would it work? Could he control aging? He would see in about thirty-six hours. So, Zeke headed out the door, planning on returning tomorrow morning.

As Zeke walked to his car, the hollow feeling in his chest returned. He literally ached from his sorrow, almost feeling like he had caught the flu. He started his electric Prius and headed for home.

As he turned down Reed Street, he marveled at its tree-lined beauty, with its neat mid-'90s colonials lined up one after the other But he noticed the yards were becoming less kept up and some cars that obviously did not work any longer were in driveways just sitting there. Jane had loved this neighborhood, made up some fellow scientists, doctors, teachers, lawyers, some small business owners and blue-collar workers. It was a good mix, but it seemed on the surface to be unraveling. As he eased the car into his driveway, his sense of loneliness and loss was overwhelming. He stared but could not go in. Instead, he backed out of the driveway and drove downtown, to a small pub where he'd stopped occasionally on his way home from the lab or where he used to meet Jane sometimes.

He did not want to go to any of the fancy restaurants or trendy bars that he and Jane used to frequent. He did not want to see anyone he knew. But this one place, more down-to-earth than the rest, was bearable.

He entered the Town Talk by the side door that led directly into the bar area. There were five or six people sitting around a large horseshoe-shaped bar. He grabbed a seat by himself at the far end of the bar. The barmaid, Wendy, recognized him from other visits and approached him with a broad smile and the inevitable, "What'll you have?" Zeke finished the sentence in his mind by saying "sailor." Jane had always laughed when he added that.

"A perfect Manhattan please, with a cherry," Zeke said. "Coming right up, Doctor. Crown Royal, right?" Wendy asked. "Crown Royal, yes." Zeke said, painfully thinking of Jane ordering her favorite drink. He sat back in the bar stool and allowed his mind to flow in and around his memories of Jane. He was working to hold back his tears when Wendy arrived with his drink.

She looked at him and said, "I'm sorry for your loss, Doc. We all are. We loved Jane. She was a beautiful person. You know me, you, and Jane had some good conversations over the years. I so admired her—admired both of you. You were such a beautiful couple."

Zeke couldn't answer, just nodded his thanks. Wendy left him alone. Her couple of years of experience as a bartender had taught her when someone wanted to tell her their life story and when they wanted to drink in peace and quiet. Still, she was being paid to keep an eye on him.

After about two hours and two Manhattan's later, Zeke's personal limit, he paid the tab, thanked Wendy, and headed for the door. Right before he exited, a tall distinguished black fellow came up to him and gently touched his arm.

"Dr. Leonard, our benefactor has asked me to express the deepest of sympathies on the passing of your wife Jane. Please accept our condolences." "Thank you," Zeke said, a little startled by the man's approach. "Excuse me, but do I know you?" Zeke asked.

"No, not at all, but my benefactor is also yours. Our benefactor became aware of your loss, and our benefactor wanted me to express our deepest sympathies. Our benefactor was keenly aware of the wonderful relationship you two shared." Zeke was taken aback by this sudden meeting. How did this man know he was even in this bar? Was he being watched? Who was "our" benefactor? Zeke noticed the man did not use the word he or she, just "our benefactor."

"Is our benefactor having me followed or watched?" Zeke asked.

"I do not know any of our benefactors' habits," was the reply. "I cannot confirm or deny anything relating to our benefactor because I have never met our benefactor. I can only say that I received a message to meet you in thirty minutes at this address. I live in Nashua, so our benefactor knew I could get here on short notice. I, too, express my sympathies. I will now depart, following our benefactors' instructions."

And with that the man turned and walked away.

Zeke exited the pub with him and watched him walk around the corner. Zeke didn't know why but he immediately liked this person. He heard an engine start and a black sedan leave quickly up the street. Zeke noted the professionalism of the man. His kind eyes. Zeke had decided not to challenge the man for more information. He could see that he had his instructions and that he probably had little if any other information. After all, Zeke's benefactor, while anonymous, had been a hundred percent supportive for ten years, with absolutely no interference. Why rock the boat now? Zeke drove slowly home and pulled into his driveway. He turned off his car and stared at the side door. He reclined his seat. He would sleep in the car tonight. Maybe tomorrow he could go into their house.

CHAPTER 4

# Can this Dog Hunt?

Zeke awoke, stiff and a little cold, at 5:00 a.m. the next morning. He stared at the side entrance for five minutes. Nature called. Okay, he thought, I will go in.

Zeke entered the neat little colonial by the homier side door. It led through a small family room, originally a breezeway that Zeke had turned into a sitting area with a wood burning stove and TV. It's where Jane and he would often sit in the evenings, watching old family shows like *Little House on the Prairie*. It was fun and corny, too. Jane would make some popcorn, and they would snuggle up and "veg" out.

The room now looked small, very, very empty . . . and cold. Zeke ran upstairs to the bathroom. He quickly stripped down and got in the shower. Maybe a hot shower would give him some relief from his pain. It did not. He dried himself off and entered their bedroom. Everything was neat except where Zeke had jumped out of the bed several days ago to go to Jane's funeral. He dressed quickly and exited the house, hurrying to get back to the lab. As he pulled the side door shut, the thought went through his mind: It is so lonely now.

*Do I ever want to come back here*? He stopped at Dunkin Donuts and got a sausage, egg, and cheese sandwich on a croissant and a tall iced tea, his daily breakfast. He sat in his car and ate his breakfast sandwich in silence. What awaited him in the lab?

Zeke unlocked the door of the lab. As he walked in, he could hear his equipment still operating in a steady humming sound. He checked the gene equipment manipulating the epigenetic marks in a cell. Would it work? Zeke thought it might.

As the equipment ceased operating, Zeke looked in the "birthing chamber." There lay a fully mature dog. Had the CRISPR manipulated the genes to the point the dog would start out as a healthy, strong, mature animal, but then have its organs age and die in a rapid manner as happened before? Zeke opened the device and out bounded a happy dog.

He noticed something important. This dog did not have a scar on its nose, as its DNA replica did. The dog appeared to be the age he wanted the dog to be. The dog was of an age before the neighbor's dog had a fight and was scarred. It looked about three years old. Not the eight years old of the neighbor's dog at present.

He needed to examine the dog's teeth, conduct some x-rays, and take some skin samples to see if he had accomplished his target. Zeke took the animal to the adjacent room where he could conduct this study.

Six hours later it was confirmed. The dog, by all test markers, was about three-years-old, exactly as Zeke had set his equipment.

Zeke took the dog, which was a purebred Labrador retriever, out of the lab and had him jump into his car. Just as he was loading the dog into the car, Martha pulled in next to him.

"Hi, Doctor. I left my sunglasses in the office yesterday, on the chair. How did your work go? Oh, what a beautiful dog. Is he yours?"

Zeke was puzzled by her question, then quickly realized she referred to his new creation.

"Yes," Zeke said, giving the dog a pat. "All mine."

"I didn't know you owned a dog. You never mentioned him."

"Well, I keep him at home in the backyard when at work. But I felt like I needed some company today."

"How did your experiment go?" Martha asked.

"Not so good, Martha. Back to the drawing board. I am going to take some time off. I will call you when I am ready to start up again. You'll be paid in full until I get back."

"Oh, Doctor, that's too much. You don't need to do that. This is a part-time job to keep me out of trouble. Henry took good care of me." Henry was Martha's husband, a local lawyer who did well before he passed away a number of years ago from cancer.

"No, I insist. I'll be in touch," Zeke said as he jumped into his car. They waved to each other as he drove off. He headed towards a large farm about ten miles outside of town. The fields had been left fallow. Long grass was growing as far as the eye could see, with trees marking the field's perimeter way off in the distance. Zeke let the dog out of the car, and it took off. What a beautiful animal. Its brown and white markings stood out in the field of green.

Suddenly there was a squawking, and about a dozen pheasants flew out of the grass with the dog gleefully chasing them into the air. Zeke thought, this dog could hunt.

Eight months passed. Zeke had not returned to the lab. He kept busy writing and rewriting his lab notes at home. He also visited with Wendy at the town talk and they created a nice friendship, even coming over to Zeke's to cook dinner for both of them. There was a twenty-three-year age gap so Zeke took on the role of a mentor to Wendy.

Martha had informed Zeke months ago that she had to keep busy, so she had taken a part-time job in a local mall as a salesclerk. She said she would come back whenever he was ready. During this time Zeke also continued to observe his subject. He had taken the dog three times to different vets to have a full examination. He explained he was thinking of buying the dog and wanted a complete physical done on the animal, including blood work and x-rays. Each report came back describing a healthy three-year-old Labrador retriever.

In fact, they said they had never seen such a beautiful healthy animal. Zeke continued to review the techniques he had used in creating this wonderful specimen.

He reread his careful, technical notes, and from them he created a massive, three-hundred-page manual on how to clone creations to be born at a certain age.

In it, he documented in laborious detail how he had modified the Wilcott equipment and built other equipment to accomplish this feat. Using the methods, he described, not only could a person recreate an existing life but could determine its age at birth. It was, he mused, a manual he could be ostracized and even cursed for creating. But he did put certain aspects of his report in a code so that only he could understand the full process.

This code was his firewall. He waited another four months, until it had been a full year since the dog was created.

The animal and its organs were stable. The year spent observing his subject, writing his detailed manual, and grieving for his lost Jane was finished. Only then did he feel safe naming the dog: Phoenix.


CHAPTER 5

# What's Next?

At this point Zeke was not sure what his next step should be. He had proven his theory that another creature could be created from a fertilized embryo with specific DNA in an artificial birthing chamber. But he had done more than that. He had taken it further. Using an artificial birthing chamber, he could take specific DNA and create that being again and again, at any age it had previously lived—at least, that was the logical extension of what he had done so far.

It was a remarkable breakthrough, especially for a single scientist to have developed, working in isolation. But Zeke was concerned. If the process he had now described in his manual was deviated from in the slightest, the resulting creature could be doomed to a short life and a terrible death. Was he ready to release it to the scientific community and the world?

Then the big question occurred to Zeke—specifically to the rigorously scientific aspect of his mind: Could the process he had invented really work on humans? Did he need to know that so that he could prevent it from being done by someone else?

A dog is not a person. He struggled with the ethics of what he was thinking. He reasoned if he conducted this experiment on a chimpanzee and saw success, he would then know how to stop it so that no one could hijack his discovery for the wrong reasons. Jane had recognized the potential horrors of his work.

To stop those horrors from materializing he had to know if it could be done in the first place. *This* was a way to protect his research and to find out if he needed to create some safeguards, some "trap doors" to stop any improper use. Was he really ready for the next step? Should he try this? After a brief struggle with his conscience, he put his curious, creative instincts in control and decided to move ahead. He *had* to know.

"All I will need is a swab from his mouth. Do you think that is possible?" Zeke asked the zookeeper.

"Coco is a pretty docile chimp, so she will cooperate with me in that. I'm happy to help you with your study of . . . what did you say you were doing, Doctor?"

"I am conducting studies on chimpanzee diseases, to see if they carry a gene in their DNA that can lead to some deadly diseases. If I can flag them, then we can manipulate their rogue gene in utero and prevent the disease before it happens. I notice that Coco has a large scar on her abdomen. What is that from?"

"Oh, she had a tumor on her liver and had surgery to remove it." "Can you recall when that operation occurred?" Zeke asked. Getting that date would give him his marker.

"Last summer, in July as I remember it. She is eight years old. She had the surgery around her seventh birthday, which would have been on July 23 last year."

As they opened the door to the chimps' home, Coco came over and greeted her caretaker with a big hug. Then she motioned for him to sit on a chair and sat on his lap.

Coco then stroked Zeke's face softly and smiled. Zeke took out a swab. The caretaker suggested Zeke do his mouth first, so Coco could see what he was doing. Coco watched with rapt attention and then opened her jaws in cooperation, displaying an intimidating mouthful of sharp teeth and fangs. She let him take the swab, then effortlessly swung herself up to the top of a tree in her pen.

Zeke took that DNA swab back to the lab, which he had not visited since last year. Being there again felt liking visiting an old friend. He had called Martha to come in, and she was delighted to hear from him. She had now largely fully retired from work, but she said she would be happy to run the spinney thing for him again.

She was waiting for him when he arrived. "How nice to see you again, Doctor. How have you been?"

"I have regained some of my equilibrium, Martha, but I still miss Jane terribly. I guess I always will," Zeke said. "I'll never be the person I was before her death. Still, work takes my mind off the loss. Thank you for helping me today.”

“I understand the loss. I miss Henry every day. How could I not help? Paying me, as you did, while you were taking a break, was too generous.”

Zeke walked over to his desk in the middle of the room. He opened the drawer and took out a key that would be used to activate the equipment to start his next experiment.

“How is your dog doing? What is his name?” Martha asked. “He is a joy. I called him . . . I call him Phoenix. I got him from the pound. I kind of brought him back from death and saved him, so to speak.”

“That’s just like you. How nice for you to have him as a companion.”

With his equipment, he created the DNA markers he needed for the fertilized chimpanzee embryo. He and Martha worked nine hours checking and rechecking the equipment. All seemed in order and ready for use. A chimpanzee has close to 98.4 percent the same DNA as humans.

By using Coco as his next experiment, he could see if the unthinkable was possible. He would set his equipment to create another Coco prior to her surgery, 7 years 6 months old. Zeke moved quickly to the birthing chamber and started it up. Martha was at her position on the other side of the equipment, more than twenty feet away.

As Zeke gave her his sign to engage the Wilcott equipment, she stepped back and watched this large piece of equipment come to life.

"Would you like me to stay after I insert the embryo and DNA sample, Doctor?"

"There's no need, thank you, Martha. This experiment will take about twenty hours and twelve minutes, by my calculations. So, that is a long time to wait. I am good from here, Martha. I'll call you for lunch soon, and we can catch up."

While Zeke had been a good and generous employer, he was so focused on his work that she could not imagine him making small talk over lunch with her. She knew this offer was just a kind gesture and that nothing would come of it. She interpreted his comment as meaning that she could and should leave now— perhaps never to return.

"I'll send you a check for your services today, Martha," Zeke said absentmindedly.

Martha, as usual, picked up her sweater and purse from the chair and left quietly, again not sure she would work with Zeke again.

After Martha had left, and she had inserted the DNA sample into the birthing chamber, he decided there was nothing else to do here until tomorrow. He was hungry, so he stopped at his little Town Talk Pub.

The lunch crowd was light, making it possible to sit at the bar and eat. He noticed his favorite barmaid and friend Wendy and gave her a pleasant hello. She always made sure she waited on him. Wendy was thinking of going back to school, and Zeke was happy to give her some insights to the world of scientific research. She was extremely interested in his work, asking all kinds of questions, which he answered to a certain point.

Zeke was happy to have someone to talk to over this past year. "What will you have?" she asked, and Zeke again finished the question in his head with, "sailor."

"I'll have a chicken salad sandwich with a beer, please, Wendy."

"Coming up," Wendy said as she walked away. "You got it."

Letting his mind return to his work, Zeke wondered, and not for the first time, what the heck he was doing. If he created this chimp before its surgery, he would have created a life from a life, born on a specific date and time, and a chimp was as close to a human being as he would go.

This was as far as he goes, he thought firmly. A chimp would prove his invention could work on humans. But what does he do with all of this, still try to offer his equipment to help the world's food supply?

It had started out as something else . . . but wait. He stopped himself. The only thing that was different from when he started this whole project, way back at Waltham Scientific, was that then his goal had been to clone an animal, speeding up the gestation time in his artificial womb to just a few hours. His idea back then had been to help address global food shortages. He had not been thinking about clones being born on a specific date, relative to specific events in their lives.

That was a big difference.

His idea had grown past that original goal. Project creep, they used to call it in college. *What good can come of this?* Zeke found himself wondering. Could he create a firewall so no one else could repeat his process, if the chimp survived? He thought of

Jane. She would not want any part of it. God knows what she would do if he thought he could bring her back, and she learned she had been "recreated" from her DNA. No, his work was going in a dangerous direction.

He faced that fact squarely. He was walking too close to the edge of ethical boundaries.

So, what positive purpose *could* his invention be put to, toward his desire to help humanity? These and many other thoughts raced through Zeke's mind that afternoon. He finally decided. He resolved that after this experiment, he was done, and the results would never see the light of day.

It was done.

He simply was not sure he could create a firewall, and it was too risky to chance. Jane spirit was back helping him, giving him wise counsel. With a sense of relief, he could almost feel her presence. He finished his sandwich and headed for the door. He was so happy and relieved with his decision that he hugged Wendy goodbye and said he'd call her later. They had talked a lot over the last year about her life and dreams, and he liked her. She was only 29 and she felt like the daughter he and Jane never had.

As he exited into the bright New England sunshine of fall, he almost collided with his benefactor's messenger.

"We have to stop meeting like this. What's your name, by the way?" Zeke asked.

"Jim Robinson, Zeke. It is not my idea to meet this way. I got a call fifteen minutes ago. Our benefactor would like to meet you after you have completed your current experiment. Our benefactor would like you to go to terminal 22B at the Manchester

Airport and board a private jet. From there all your travel needs will be taken care of by our benefactor."

Zeke wanted to say that he was not going anywhere without knowing what this meeting was all about. But he stopped himself. He knew what he was going to do and what the meeting would be about. He did owe it to the benefactor to notify him in person of this final decision to end this project, with no return on investment.

Eleven years of work and fifteen million dollars up in smoke. *Just go*, Zeke told himself. *Then it will be over.*

"Let our benefactor know that I can travel in one month. It will take me that long to make sure my experiment is stable. So, let us set the date for November 20th."

"I will pass on your message,"

"Have you met this person yet, Jim?"

"No, I haven't Zeke. I don't know who he or she is. But whoever it is has supported my project for almost 4 years now. It's complete, so I expect I will be summoned someday soon too." Zeke found talking to Jim to be an unusual and pleasant experience. You were immediately drawn in by his sincerity and kindness in his voice. He was the type of person Zeke would like to be friends with. They chatted for another 10 minutes or so getting to know a bit more about each other. Zeke learned that Jim has been involved in politics most of his adult life and now at 50 was working on a project that he hoped would transform politics as we know it. Jim, in general terms, expressed his deep concern for the direction the country was going in and the abject poverty that these new government policies were creating. It sounded fascinating but something Zeke knew little about. Zeke simply never paid attention to what was happening to his country around him.

They shook hands and promised each other they would be in touch after exchanging numbers.

Zeke travelled home, stumbled into the living room. He made himself a perfect Manhattan and slumped in his chair. He thought he did notice and read somewhere where the country was in a lot of political and financial turmoil. He sipped on his drink and finished it. He was simply emotionally and physically spent and fell face first on the couch, exhausted. He immediately fell asleep. He forgot to set his alarm for a 2:00 am wake up call.

At 4:00 a.m. the next morning Zeke woke up with a start. He hurried upstairs, took off his clothes, took a quick shower, and dressed in his laboratory blues. He had slept past the finish time on his equipment. It shut off automatically, but he would have preferred to have been there when it had finished. He jumped into his electric car and put it in reverse.

He still got a kick out of how the car would start to move, making no noise. As he passed down Reed Street, he noticed the bright reds and yellows of the leaves starting to display their beauty. *It is fall,* he thought. Jane loved this time of the year. It would raise her naturally joyful spirit to a whole new level of exuberance.

God, how he missed her so much, every day. Would it ever lessen? Would the hurt ever stop? He'd see her again he thought.

In fifteen minutes, he was at the lab. Its big green steel door caught the light from the early morning sunrise. What was waiting inside for him?

Slowly Zeke took out the key and turned the lock. The door swung open easily and he entered. The equipment had automatically stopped about an hour before his arrival. An awful screeching was coming from the birthing chamber, as if someone were being murdered. He reached for a baseball bat that had long been propped, untouched, in the corner of the lab.

He drew towards the screeching noises, towards the banging and screaming. As he got to the birthing chamber, he looked in through a glass viewer. He saw that his creature was awake and wanted out. The chimp was mad, really mad. Zeke slowly cracked the door. The chimp's hand and fingers grabbed it and shoved it open with the power of ten men.

Out leaped the chimp, right onto Zeke's face, biting and scratching. In an instant, Zeke's left ear was gone. Coco grabbed a hold of one of his eyes and plucked it out like a plum from a pie. Zeke screamed in pain, grabbing his face. Coco bit into his scalp and nearly ripped it right off. Zeke staggered. He was bleeding profusely from his wounds, and he stumbled back, in too much shock even to feel pain. Blood was everywhere, gushing from his face and head.

The chimp suddenly jumped onto a nearby table, it's back to Zeke. Its coat glistened with sweat and Zeke's blood. Its shoulders were hunched. Slowly it raised its head and turned and looked over its shoulder at Zeke. It screeched a primal cry, turned its head further, and looked again at its creator. Its eyes bore into Zeke's one eye that was left. Coco was going to rip that one out too.

The chimp curled up its lip and bared its teeth, and the long fangs Zeke had noticed at the zoo looked larger than ever. Coco screeched again, even louder this time, turned, and leaped at Zeke. Even in his debilitated, semi-blind state, Zeke understood that this was the moment of life or death. The chimp, with its superior strength, was going to rip him apart.

As the creature turned and leapt, it gave Zeke just a second to raise the bat that was still in his hand. Just as the chimp leaped, Zeke swung a baseball bat as hard as he could with both hands. He connected with the side of the animal's head, with a sound like a watermelon being smashed on the floor.

Coco fell with a thud to the floor, stunned, blood gushing from its ears, suddenly quiet and still, after the mayhem.

Zeke could barely breathe or move, with blood running into his mouth, his nose split in two, and his injuries and shock shutting down all his faculties. But he somehow summoned the strength to drag himself over to the chimp's form, a mass on the floor, and beat in the animal's head with a maniac intensity he did not know he possessed. He swung the bat until he could no longer lift his arms.

The animal quivered violently as it died, its brains splattered everywhere.

Zeke slumped to the floor. There was no time left for an ambulance. The chimp had killed him. Zeke's body just didn't fully understand it yet, but Zeke's mind did. He pulled himself up from the floor and reached for a glass mixing dish from the desk drawer.

He staggered over to the storage containers neatly marked with DNA from many species. He removed the lid of his own frozen DNA. Then he raised his fertilized human embryo from its -80-degree freezer. He put the samples in a small piece of equipment he designed to bring these samples to room temperature quickly without destroying their integrity. In thirty seconds, it rang as it finished. It seemed like an eternity to Zeke.

He was fading. He reached in and got out the samples. With shaking hands, he put them both in the birthing dish and closed the lid. He was trying to get over the Wilcott Equipment now to start it, but he was fainting, failing fast. He fell to the floor and knew he was not going to be able to get up. It was over. It was all over. He was comforted with the thought he would be with Jane again. He smiled.

Lying on the floor staring at the ceiling with one eye he felt at peace, and he saw . . . was that Martha? She was stoic. No screaming, no emotion. No longer the brilliant and sweet grandmother who helped him in the past, but a soldier. She quickly grabbed the sample from Zeke's twitching hand. She had been watching from the moment he entered the lab. Zeke's benefactor had called her and told her to get over to the lab and wait outside for Zeke to arrive.

The benefactor said she should be ready to help if needed, but to keep her distance. While waiting outside she heard the screams and then her cell phone rang. She was told to go to the lab and do what she could. Martha started the equipment. She took the samples and stared at them, as the rest of the equipment hummed into action.

"God forgive me for what I am about to do," Martha said silently and gave herself the sign of the cross. She slid the samples into the birthing chamber. She turned and watched as Zeke's body heaved up for one final breath and stopped.

Quickly she went to where she had laid down her sweater on her chair. She put it over her shoulders and walked out of the lab.

**CHAPTER 6**

[47]

# It's Over When It's Over

Zeke was gone. Coco had ripped the life out of him in about thirty seconds. He bled to death, a victim of his own creation. His mistake was he was not there when the animal awoke, found itself in an enclosure 7 feet long, 5 feet wide, and 3 feet high, and freaked out. From all the hair and blood found inside the birthing chamber, it was clear that Coco was in a rage and a frenzy when Zeke opened the door.

Little good that did Zeke, now as he laid on the floor next to the chimp's body. He stared blindly at the ceiling, with his one remaining eye, as his life ebbed away.

Two days later, exactly at forty-eight hours and ten minutes, Zeke crawled out of the same birthing chamber. He did not know where it was, why he was naked, and what those two lumps of rotting flesh were on the floor. He looked around this laboratory. He had never been here before. He saw some lockers. He hurried over to one and opened it. Empty.

The next one, however, had clothes hanging neatly on hooks. He slipped on the underwear, pants, and shirt, which fit him perfectly. The sneakers fit, too. Now that he was dressed, he just stared at the room, wondering where he was and what was going on? Where was everybody?

He decided to take a closer look at the bodies in front of this equipment.

Except for the Wilcott equipment, which he was working on right now at his job at Waltham Scientific, he recognized nothing. From what he could see there was a corpse of a person, maybe a man, lying in his lab blues next to the battered body of a chimpanzee. Blood that had pooled on the floor had dried. He saw a cardboard box in the corner and flattened it out to use as a mat, as he kneeled to get a closer view of the human form. It looked like the man had been in a violent accident or attack, with the face and hair pretty much gone.

He reached into the man's pocket and found first some keys, then a worn billfold.

He opened the leather wallet and drew in his breath sharply in surprise. There on the driver's license he saw his own picture and his own name. He quickly grabbed a credit card, and it had his name on it, too. With increasing agitation, he reached in the other pocket and found the man's cell phone. It was a much more modern phone than the flip phone he had. It was locked, and he had no idea of the pass code.

But he tried the one he used, and it worked. He dropped them on the floor baffled.

He stood slowly and looked around, trying to sort out these many impossibilities, to make sense of what made no sense.

There was no office, no reception area, no phone in sight. Only lab equipment and one chair in the corner. What was going on? Where was he? Who is this dead person on the floor with his IDs and a newfangled phone in his pocket? What was this equipment he had crawled out of? Had he been kidnapped and just escaped from a cell? He needed to call Jane.

He decided he would get the heck out of this lab now. He needed to see Jane. They had been married only a couple of years, and they called each other several times a day. Maybe she was looking for him.

As he exited the large green steel door, Jim Robinson walked up to him and asked, "Dr. Leonard, are you alright? Our benefactor called me and said you had an emergency and that I needed to go to your lab and wait for you to exit. I have been here for about two hours. Our benefactor said that they needed your notes on the table, from the left side of the lab table. But that I was not to go into your lab itself. I was just to get you and the notes, and then I was to leave with you to Florida."

"My benefactor? My lab? Notes? Florida? I have no idea what you are talking about. I don't know you, and there is no way I am going anywhere with you. I need to call my wife. There are dead bodies in that lab. I don't have any idea what is going on here."                "Our benefactor thought that this might happen, so if you don't mind," Jim turned and gestured to two large men waiting in the shadows, who rushed past him and grabbed Zeke.

They injected him with a needle, and before Zeke could say stop, he was out.

One of the large men stepped stealthily into the lab and grabbed the notes. He exited quickly. The three men and Zeke left in a large black SUV. As they got into the SUV, a crew of five people got out of another panel truck, parked nearby. This other crew was wearing full white hooded coveralls from their feet to the tops of their heads, with their faces hidden by protective masks.

They entered the lab with industrial-strength cleaning chemicals and equipment, of the type used to sanitize houses and apartments after murders.

In four hours, they would leave the lab perfectly clean and in order, as if nothing had happened there. From Zeke's body, they removed his wedding ring and watch, collecting them with Zeke's wallet and phone, which lay on the floor. They then carried out two bulky body bags and took them to a local crematory, where they were destroyed.

That was the end of Zeke #1, the elder man.

When Zeke #2, the younger man, awoke, he was startled to find himself on a private jet. The two men who had abducted him were sitting on either side of him. Facing him was Jim Robinson, the man who had addressed him when he left the lab. "Don't be frightened. You are safe. We are here to protect you and help you understand what is going on," Jim said as calmly and reassuringly as he could.

Zeke looked around quickly and saw that he had no option but to listen.

A lady came over and asked him if he would like a cold drink of water or an alcoholic beverage. Perhaps a perfect Manhattan she asked, with a cherry? How did she know that was "their" drink?

Zeke did not recognize that the flight attendant was Wendy from the pub he had recently visited. Wendy, whom he had hugged only a few days ago.

Jim noticed these blank looks Zeke was giving people and was puzzled. Zeke did not seem to recognize him either. He had given Zeke messages from their mutual benefactor by the pub on two occasions and just had a nice conversation with him.

Why? Was he in shock? He seemed disoriented when he exited the lab. Did he have a head injury that had left his memory impaired? What were the dead bodies he had been speaking of? In speculating on possible causes, Jim did not guess the real reason: that this Zeke had not met him yet.

Jim Robinson had his instructions from their benefactor on what to do when Zeke woke up, and he followed them exactly, saying, "You are to read the following summary, Doctor. It is for your eyes only. Please take a seat at the back of the plane and read this. Once you do, I am told you will have a better understanding of what has transpired in your life. I do not know anything beyond what I have just told you. I am telling you that so you do not get frustrated, asking me questions I cannot answer for you. I know nothing of your work. All I can emphasize to you is that you are among friends, and you are perfectly safe."

Zeke decided to take Jim's advice and read the thick report that was now being handed to him. It was sealed to prevent anyone from sneaking a peek undiscovered. Zeke got up and went to the back of the plane. The flight attendant, Wendy, brought him a glass of water, which Zeke gulped down. He did not realize how thirsty he was. It was like he had never drank water before, which he had not. It made him feel like a new man, which he was. As she left to get him more water, he tore open the package. It started as follows:

*Dr. Leonard—You have been working on a way to regenerate life by using fertilized embryos and DNA in an artificial womb. You have been working in your laboratory for the last eleven years on this effort. The reason you do not remember this work is that YOU are a creation of your efforts.*

What did these words mean?

Zeke repeated them over and over to himself—*I am a creation of my own efforts*—trying to absorb them. For the next hour he read through the many materials in the package. It contained d monthly reports of his progress and his thoughts on his next steps. He read about needing millions of dollars to continue his research and about receiving it from his benefactor. The report was made up of his own words reviewing his work. He understood it all but remembered nothing. Did he have amnesia? Was he able to use a fertilized embryo and DNA to create life at any stage of the subject's life in an accelerated period of time? Finally, he got to the last page.

*On October 22, you endeavored to use chimpanzee DNA to see if your experiment would work on that level of biological physiology. Unfortunately, your subject chimp emerged from the birthing chamber in an enraged state and attacked you. You were able to defend yourself, but you had been mortally wounded. You knew that your only possibility of survival would be to recreate yourself, which is what you tried to do before you died. You were successful. As you have read, you can set the period in one's life to regenerate life from the subject's DNA. In your weakened state you set your time of recreation at a younger age than when you passed. That is why you do not remember any of these events, since they have not existed yet for you, in your new mind and body of approximately thirty-three years of age. You were fifty-three years old when you died. We realize these circumstances would be a shock for anyone, even a scientist like yourself. So please take time to absorb what has happened, and we can discuss these events further when you arrive at my home. We are*

Zeke sat there stunned. Could all that he had just read possibly be true?

Had his life fast-forwarded backward so that he had just lost more than twenty years of it? He had no firsthand knowledge of what the older Zeke had been doing in those years, only what he, the younger, had learned from reading those reports. Now on the airplane, he felt like himself, not a replica of himself, but the scientific reviews of the independent work "he" had been doing—the years of updates and reports on it—we're almost too much to believe.

They read more like science fiction.

Though he had always wanted to explore DNA and its possibilities, he was currently being stymied by the management at Waltham Scientific. He was planning to try to persuade his boss to allow his team to at least poke around in this area of study. Evidently, he doesn't work at Waltham Scientific anymore. He had not been able to persuade Waltham Scientific, and he'd been fired?

And set up an independent lab? His work was meticulously outlined by him, the equipment modifications and the new machines he built from scratch were all there.

He could see that these modifications would have taken years of painstaking work. What does Jane think about this direction his life took? Does Jane know where he is? He needed to call her. She would be worried sick that he had disappeared with no trace. Zeke leaped from his seat.

"I need to call my wife," he said in an urgent voice to Jim. "Do you have a phone I can use? Don't worry, I understand a bit better now what is going on. I will tell her only that I am on a sudden business trip out of town to meet with an investor, which is true. I don't want her to be concerned when I don't come home."

Jim Robinson stared at Zeke. He was told this might happen. Jim had expressed his condolences to Zeke well over a year ago. He hesitated.

"What's wrong?" Zeke asked. "I told you, I understand now what I was working on. And approximately what happened. Those bodies were chimpanzees I had been working on, but something went wrong. I just need to be in touch with my wife, Jane, to let her know where I am so she will not think I have suddenly disappeared."

Jim proceeded to follow his instruction, using simple, direct words and sticking to what little he knew.

"My name is Jim Robinson," he said. "I live in Nashua, too. We have met several times over the past year or so. You have met our stewardess, Wendy, many times as well, at your neighborhood pub and you have become friends," Jim said, pointing to her. "I was told you would not remember any of our meetings for some reason that I don't understand. And I hate to do this, but I have been instructed what to tell you if you ask about your wife. You, you . ." he stopped, catching his breath. "Your wife passed away from a heart attack over a year ago. I saw you after the funeral to express my condolences. I am sorry, Zeke. I am so sorry to have to tell you this."

Zeke just stood there stunned, disbelieving.

"No. That is not possible. She is a young and healthy person. She is only 33 years old. What are you saying? I just left her this morning for work in Waltham. She was alive and fine. You must be wrong. Let me call my house, please." Jim handed Zeke a phone.

Zeke quickly dialed his number at home. Unknown to the present Zeke, the older Zeke had changed the home voicemail greeting about six months after his wife's death, feeling it was just too painful for her parents to hear her voice when they called the house. As soon as Zeke heard his voice on the message, rather than Jane's, he knew that what Jim had said was true.

Zeke would never have changed her voicemail message. He loved her voice as he loved every fiber of her being. So, she was gone?

His mind did not want to believe this terrible news. Still, he believed she was indeed gone, the second he heard his own voice on the phone. Zeke collapsed to his knees and put his face in his hands. He was shaking uncontrollably.

He started with a quiet moaning that melded into sobbing. His heart broke all over again, for the first time in this new Zeke's, the younger man's chest.

# CHAPTER 7

# It Ain't Over Yet

Zeke stumbled to the back of the plane, blinded with grief. His beautiful wife of only three years was gone. She had opened up his life to enjoy so much more of the world that he had never appreciated before. He was simply stunned by this news. About one hour after this revelation the plane landed in West Palm Beach, Florida. There was a private hangar that the plane slowly rolled into. Jim told him it was time to go and he helped him to his feet. Jim was such a caring individual. Zeke slowly descended the stairs with a heavy heart, still in shock.

A limousine was waiting nearby. He turned to Jim and asked. "How old was my wife when she died, Jim?"

"Her obituary said she was forty-nine years old, Zeke."

"That means we were married eighteen years. How did she die?" Zeke whispered.

"She died instantly, from a heart attack. She never knew what happened. She was loved by hundreds of people, Zeke. Her passing was mourned by many, many people." Jim said.

Zeke slipped into the limo and settled back in its rich leather seats. The car felt like a spacious, luxurious tank, with heavy doors and thick, bullet-proof glass. It was big enough in the back to seat at least six people comfortably.

A sound-proof glass partition separated the passenger and driver areas. The driver now opened this divider with the press of a button and, saying, "I believe these are yours, sir," handed him a wedding ring, watch, cellphone, and wallet. Zeke took out his license and looked again at the picture of his older self, as he had when kneeling by the body on the bloody floor of the lab. This time he flipped down a mirror from the ceiling and compared his present self with the photo.

He couldn't believe his eyes. He was so old in the official little laminated picture. Now he was young again, the hands of time having been turned back.

Jim did not get in the car with him. Leaning down to speak to Zeke—the man, the mirror image, and a smiling, oblivious figure in the license photo—he said, "I was asked to deliver you this far, Zeke. Now I am heading back home."

"How are you connected with the person I am going to see?" Zeke asked.

"Our benefactor has given me over four million dollars in the past four years on a project I have been working on. Beyond that, I have been asked not to say too much about it, but I can tell you it is of national importance. This person, whoever he or she is, has America's well-being at heart. My job has been to help our country's progress, which has been fully supported by this individual. I will meet this person next month for the first time, and I am looking forward to doing so. I have an idea who it is, but I guess I will just have to wait until next month. Good luck, Zeke. Godspeed. Until we meet again."

And with that Jim turned and ascended the stairs back into the jet.

The limo pulled out of the airport hangar with a police escort of two motorcycle cops. "Where the heck am I being taken?" Zeke thought to himself. Why is a police escort needed? He was still grappling with news of Jane's death and the fact he had lived to be more than fifty, then died, then came back to life, younger, but having missed a big chunk of his life. He was wondering all over again on how he would live his life without Jane.

The ride lasted about forty minutes. Finally, the car pulled up to the most grand and lavish mansion he had ever seen. The place was enormous, with every detail saying, "wealth".

A doorman greeted him, saying, "Welcome to Mar-a-Lago, Dr. Leonard. Please follow me."

"Mar-a-Lago" was elaborately written above the arch to the main lobby. Zeke's mind spun only with bewildered questions.

"I am at Donald Trump's residence in Florida? Why would a real estate baron and host from a TV show want to see me about a scientific research project? Is he funneling his money into my project? Why? What for? For a new game show?"

As he was ushered through this massive hotel lobby, Zeke saw gold embossing everywhere, luxurious and shining.

The lobby was filled only with wealthy men and women and those who waited on them. Many men were dressed for golf and the ladies in expensive brands of summer outfits. There were maids, butlers, staff, and security guards everywhere. This place was about as high end as it went. Zeke was guided to an elevator that took him to the top floor.

When he emerged, two men greeted him, each with earpieces dangling from their ears. They looked a lot like a matched set of Secret Service agents, except one was slightly bigger than the other. "If we may, sir, we would like to check you for weapons," the bigger one said.

"Weapons? Are you kidding me? I don't even own a weapon."

"Sorry, sir. Standard procedure." They proceeded to frisk him with a metal detector.

"Who am I seeing? Isn't this Donald Trump's residence?" Zeke asked.

"Yes, sir. We are here to protect the former president. He wishes to meet with you," the slightly smaller of the two Secret Service agents answered.

"Former president? What former president is visiting Donald Trump? Clinton?"

The agents looked at each other. "Are you feeling alright, sir? We cannot let you in to see Mr. Trump if you are unwell."

"I am just trying to get the picture here. Wait, are you telling me Donald Trump, the host of *The Apprentice*, was also our President?"

"Wait here, sir. I'll be right back." One of the agents left, talking into his security microphone, while Zeke stood there wondering what world he had woken up in.

He felt like he was in a dream or a drug-induced hallucination. The agent returned without a word and ushered Zeke into a sumptuous room. He had visited the Palace of Versailles on a trip to France for Waltham Scientific Bioworks. This place seemed even more opulent.

"Thank you, Phil. I'll take it from here," Trump said as he entered the room. "Sit down, Zeke. I am sure all this is confusing. Make yourself comfortable."

Zeke stood there looking at a large man in front of him. It was a strange sensation to see this celebrity in the flesh, after previously having seen him only in media images. Mr. Trump was somewhat heavyset and close to 6 feet 2 inches tall. His hair was dyed an orange, blonde. Appearing much older than when on TV, he now looked to be a man well into his 80s.

"Mr. Trump, what is going on? Is this all real? Are you filming something for *The Apprentice*?"

Trump burst out laughing.

"I am afraid you have missed out on a few things. I was probably the greatest President the country has ever had—better than Lincoln, I think. That was nearly fifteen years ago. So, I think that puts you at about thirty-three years old, and you were more than fifty years old when your accident happened. Not a bad deal, picking up twenty plus years."

"You were president of the United States. That can't be!"

"Yes, well, it was. And I was a great President, probably the best there ever will be, as history will tell. Had the Democrats all over me for the whole time. They impeached me, twice the bastards, but I beat them all. That really pissed them off. They went after me so hard, with no wrongdoing, everything perfect.

"Then we had the plague. I handled that perfectly too. Warp speed. They just wanted Trump gone. So, I'm eighty-eight years old now, Zeke. You got younger, and I got older. Does not seem fair. Let's sit down and talk awhile. You've had shock after shock today. I realize you learned about Jane again today. I am so sorry you must relive that loss all over again. Sad, so sad. They called me the consoler in chief, so come on over here sit down. Have a drink. I don't drink myself but feel free. I had a perfect Manhattan made for you or just some water."

Zeke helped himself to the drink. He needed it. He took a sip, then a bigger swallow.

"Now, let's get down to business. What are we going to do with our invention?"

Zeke sipped again, almost too wiped out to speak or think. His thoughts seemed reduced to short sentences. Trump. President. Did he keep his show? "Our invention?" We are partners?

"Mr. Trump, I have no idea what I was thinking when I created this invention that I read about on the way down here. It seems to me now that I got lost along the way. The reports I read say I wanted to develop a new food source for the world. Something inexpensive that protected our environment. What I have done is create a Frankenstein. I *am* a Frankenstein. I shouldn't even be here."

"Well," Trump said thoughtfully, "Don't be so hard on yourself. If it weren't for your invention, you wouldn't be here right now, that is true. That monkey beat the crap out of you. I saw it on cameras in your lab, and I could not believe it. Vicious. More vicious than Hillary was to me. She was so bad, so bad."

"The fact that I am even alive and here is freaking me out, Mr. Trump," Zeke moaned. "I—the former I—didn't think this thing all the way through. What do you do with this invention? People could live forever. Just keep going forever. I was searching for a firewall to stop that from happening, but I don't think I ever found one. We have no right to alter God's plan. I think the lab should be destroyed and my notes along with it."

Trump got up and moved over to the huge fireplace in the room. On the mantle were pictures of Trump with every world leader.

"I can understand what you are saying. I would have no interest in having your laboratory remake me. As Mae West said, 'You only live once, and if you do it right, once is enough.' I have lived enough for five lifetimes, and I am good with that. But our country is in trouble. After I Made America Great and the Biden presidency ended a new Republican president took over. Nice lady named Joan Wilkins. Wilkins chose a guy named Bennett as her running mate. Bennett is a real communist, a socialist nut bag, but he helped Wilkins get elected since the far left loved him and Joan needed their vote. Since he could not really do anything as VP, what is the harm?

"But Wilkins died in office just after she won her second term, and this Bennett takes over."

"Out of sympathy the Congress gives him a number of legislative wins which are a disaster for our economic system. The people see politicians as just power- and wealth-seeking scumbags. And they are right. Big, big swamp. I didn't need any of their money, so they did not know what to do with me. I was never one of them. I stopped globalization from taking place, and they hated me for that. We need to get someone in office who can head the country in the right direction economically, Zeke. I tried to promote a good woman governor from Maine, but no one would listen to Trump. No one wants to here from Trump. Big mistake. They have had enough of me. Their mistake, but that's the way it is. I'm afraid these politicians are going to destroy our country from within."

Trump was clearly shaken by the problems he described. He had lost a bit of his orange color and became a little pink. Zeke could see he was deeply concerned.

"What we need is an unquestionable leader, one who can bring us together under one banner. We may disagree on policy, but we need to get the economics right. Get the government out of people's business." Trump sat down again. "Why don't you go rest in your room? I cannot imagine the mental strain you have been through. Actually, I can. Those Dems were ruthless. Let's meet for breakfast tomorrow. Do you play golf? We could play golf. I've got a beautiful course here, the best in the world."

"No, sir, I don't. But I could use the rest. I would like some time alone."

"Yes, of course. In your room is a film I put together covering the last fifteen years in this country from a political point of view. Watch it if you are up to it, and we can discuss it tomorrow."

He rang a bell, and a stately looking man entered the room.

"Peters, please show Dr. Leonard to his suite." Trump turned again to Zeke and breezily suggested, "Order food in, relax, try the lap pool in your room if you'd like. Peters will bring you to my private dining room at 10:00 a.m. tomorrow. See you then. Good night, Zeke."

"Good night, Mr. Trump," Zeke said. He still could hardly believe that Donald Trump had been the President. It seemed so unlikely. But if was one thing Zeke knew for certain, it was that the unlikely could happen.

Escorting Zeke was Malcom Peters. In old England he would be called Trump's footman. Taking care of Trump's every need. He was of average height with graying hair. He was impeccably dressed and manicured. At the elevator, they went down one floor.

"I hope you enjoy this room, sir. It is almost two thousand square feet. It has a lap pool, sauna, whirlpool, and steam room. The dining room has some hors d'oeuvres ready for you. Feel free to order whatever else you want, and the kitchen will make it for you."

"Thank you, but these extravagant offerings are not necessary. I feel drained. I just need to rest and time to think. A fancy room is not necessary for me. A normal room will do fine."

"Dr. Leonard, no one in Mr. Trump's inner orbit is any longer in a normal place. Get used to it," Peters said kindly, with surprising frankness.

He opened the twelve-foot-high solid oak door to Zeke's room, revealing a suite that was Trumpian in all its aspects and accouterments. A massive wall of windows looked out over a beautiful golf course and the sparkling Atlantic. The pool in the room was about 4 feet wide and 20 feet long. Peters showed Zeke how to start the pool so the constant stream would allow him to swim in place. In its style, the living room's decor was a combination of the sultans' Topkapi Palace in Istanbul and the emperors' Hofburg Palace in Vienna.

Zeke walked, it seemed for a mile, to his attached bedroom suite, which had a large four poster bed with a canopy of heavy red velvet.

The furnishings were dark heavy oak and mahogany, beautifully carved with heads of birds and serpents. Unusual. Zeke fell down in the bed and slowly turned over. All he could think about was Jane. What was he going to do without Jane? That hollow pit in his chest almost made him double over, and finally able to let out his emotions and tears started to roll down his cheeks.

It was dark when Zeke awoke. He lay there for another ten minutes trying to put everything in order, like the good scientist he was.

He reviewed in this mind what he knew: He was working with DNA and cloning, with the goal to create a new supply of food for the world. His notes said he had been unsuccessful in his experiments or many years, until he had a breakthrough with a dog around year ten. But the first dog was birthed as a fully mature dog *by accident*, but the subject died in just over a month. Now fascinated by this development he worked on that problem, and as he did, he stumbled upon the length of time needed to control the full maturation of his subject.

By manipulating gestation time per species, he ended up with a fully mature dog that is alive to this day. Inexplicably he moved up the animal chain to a chimpanzee.

He stared at the ceiling. What had prompted him to go off in this new direction, away from his objective? Ego?

What had happened was not in the original plan, but now it needed to be reckoned with and understood. When he was regenerating himself after the attack, he must not have set his time to the right length of time in the birthing chamber. He read in his notes that he had established a baseline for humans by using his successful dog experiment.

Turned out he wasn't "cooked" long enough to return at his original age. According to the notes, he must have cut short his regeneration time by two hours, four minutes, and nineteen seconds. Zeke had gathered from Trump yesterday—and from what he had seen himself upon awakening at the lab—that the fatal attack must have clouded his abilities at the end.

He was so bloodied and literally dying on his feet that it is a surprise he was even able to set up the equipment by himself at all. It must have been an awful scene. His notes occasionally mentioned his assistant Martha. He had no recollection of her, but the notes say several times that he kept her in the dark about his work. And his notes stated he did not truthfully explain where Phoenix had come from.

He could see no one really knew what was going on except, he assumed, Jane, and his benefactor Trump.

Zeke's thoughts now proceeded in a dark direction. What good will this invention do for humanity, except screw us all up even more? He felt he had unwittingly unleashed replicas of everyone running around at different ages, groups of people who all happen to look and act like Larry Bird on a champion basketball team, gas-lighting dictators bringing themselves back time and again to rule forever.

No, this discovery is simply too dangerous, too easy to be abused. The equipment, the notes, the video tapes that Trump must have been making—all of it had to go.

Zeke was sure that this was what he would tell Trump at breakfast. Then his mind wandered to Jane, his darling, his love.

He finally fell asleep again thinking of her, hoping to see her in his dreams.

At 8:20 a.m. Zeke awoke. He indulged in the steam room for ten minutes. He turned on the lap pool and swam in place for another ten minutes, had a shower and a shave, and started to feel better. New clothing was laid out for him. He dressed in Khaki pleated pants, a bright white shirt, blue blazer, and a new pair of D'marge loafers, too, which had been ordered for him from "The Playbook of the Modern Man" site. If "the clothes make the man," he thought, then he was moving up in the world, as he settled into a wingback chair to watch the video that Trump had provided as homework.

As it was designed to do, it caught him up on national events he had missed when he jumped forward to the present.

At 10 a.m. there was a knock at the door. Zeke answered it to find Peters, ready to guide him to his breakfast with Mr. Trump. As they walked down a long hall, Zeke noticed ceilings arching twenty feet high above him, gilded with gold paint. Gold accented all the woodwork.

He had never in his life been to a place that emitted such a sense of brazen, ostentatious, unapologetic wealth. Entering the private dining area, he saw Mr. Trump seated with a beautiful, slim woman—his wife, the former first lady, Zeke assumed. He did not know her name. Zeke figured her to be about sixty years old.

In a pronounced eastern European accent, she introduced herself as Melania and said, "Dr. Leonard, much pleasure to meet you. Donald told me much about your brilliance. I hope your accommodations comfortable?"

"Nice to meet you, Mrs. Trump," Zeke responded, bowing slightly. "Yes, my room was magnificent, thank you."

Melania then excused herself, saying she was going for a horse ride and that she hoped to see them both later.

As Zeke sat down, he noticed that the former president had over a dozen newspapers spread around him on the table and on the floor.

The headlines blared, "Violent Riots Break Out across America" and "Rule of Law Gone in America." Trump pointed to the papers and said, "It has been like this for several years now. There was much division created by the both parties while I was in office—chaos that the Dems and the fake-news media hoped would wear the American people down. Once worn down, the idea was, the people would accept anyone who offered peaceful, presidential language and an almost do-nothing administration.

But after Biden finished his presidency and when that nice Joan Wilkins died in office and her VP Bartlett took over, it was a disaster. Bartlett was not in office one month and these radical proposals started. The Second Amendment was challenged. It took two years, but eventually they got it so only pistols and shotguns were allowed. No automatic weapons at all. All other guns were confiscated, with a penalty of five years in jail if you hid one.

"There were terrible shootings everywhere as they tried to confiscate guns."

Trump paused and took a bite of a bun. He then continued with his bitter account.

"Bartlett's next action was to pass taxes and restrictions on oil and gas production and stop fracking. Trying to force a greener effort, but it was before the other industries like wind and solar were ready to replace the energy these fuels provided. The taxes were so severe that the industry nearly collapsed. Since not enough alternative energy had been created, there are blackouts and brownouts all day across the country. This energy mess affected all industries.

"Unemployment rose to over 20 percent like when I shut down the country for the pandemic in 2020. So, Congress decided under his direction to send everyone a check on a monthly basis, forever! Creating all that money fueled run-away inflation."

Another bite of bun.

"Then Bartlett's administration taxed anyone making over a million dollars a year at seventy-five percent with few deductions. So, what happens, anyone with means moves their income and business offshore. Capitalism was declared over by this Bartlett guy. He says he is running for another term. He and a good number in Congress proposed taking over as many large private businesses as they can and federalizing them. They need the income to afford all their ideas.

"Now 'the people' are supposed to own Google and Amazon and Ford and GM. People are hungry and out of work. So, what happens? People start to revolt. It's Venezuela all over again.

"I warned them that there was a group in Congress, in both parties, that wanted some of these changes, but they went too far. That's where we are now. I have talked to Bartlett several times. He seems like a good person but with a view of this country that is bad and not realistic. It has all gone wrong for the country, and when a system starts to break down, it is impossible to control. We have an election coming up in 36', and we are afraid if he wins another term, that is it for the country that most of us know. There is a chance of an armed revolution.

"That is where you come in, Zeke."

Zeke was stunned to hear of the perilous state of the nation that Trump was describing and also by his last line. What did he mean, that is "where he comes in"?

Zeke believed in a fundamentally fairer system, with more equality in income distribution, but what was being tried in the government, at least as Trump had outlined it, did not sound good. Was the former president exaggerating for effect or being paranoid or overly partisan? Look at all the wealthy people in Mar-a-Lago's lobby, who seemed to be living life as usual. Were large corporations being nationalized, at the exact same time? That would be insane and was hard to believe. That is what dictators do in repressive countries around the world. Not here. Impossible.

Over the next hour, Zeke argued with Trump, raising counterpoints and objections, saying that the picture he painted was too grim, too bleak.

Trump held firm, telling Zeke to go out and see for himself. He called in Peters and told him to give Zeke a tour of "our new world." Had Zeke known about these radical changes in American society in his "other" life? Maybe he did, but to the new Zeke, the conditions as just described were startling, if true.

As Peters and Zeke left the hotel and jumped into a waiting limo, they at first saw nothing but wealth. They were heading into Palm Beach. Zeke's first sign of any issue was as they drove down Worth Avenue. This street had been where the elite met to shop. But now many of the stores were shuttered. Broken glass littered the sidewalks from obvious break-ins. People were gathering on the corners of the street, standing and idling in small clusters. When they saw the limo, they yelled obscenities and threw cans and other debris at the car.

"Where are the police?" Zeke asked Peters.

"They come out onto the streets only if there is a murder or serious assault," he answered. "It is like the Wild West now. You're on your own out there.

"There was a riot about four months ago. It was part of dozens of riots across the country where the 'people' were attacking the 'upper class'. This place is only one of thousands of sites across the country where these attacks have happened. The *old middle class* is pissed. Black, white, Asian, Hispanic you name it. If they thought of themselves as middle class, they got angry because *they were being used* to level the playing field. Their hard work, their sacrifices no longer meant a thing.

"This socializing of our economy just did not work out the way Bartlett thought it would. But instead of backing off when so many saw his policies failing, he doubled down. You know Zeke, wealthy people always find ways to maintain their wealth. That was noticed by everyone as the general population was suffering. So, what happens? You plant the seeds of class warfare. Under all the glitz Mar-a-Largo is an armed camp. We are ending up with more equality, in the sense of equally poorer.

"And here is the rub. In the process of making all of these changes, powerful cronies were created in Congress just like in every socialist's system and they are making out like bandits. What do they call them in Russia—oligarchs? They want the unrest and turmoil to continue so they can keep raking it in. Bartlett may get re-elected and actually have the political clout to bring down the entire capitalists' system in this country."

As they continued to drive around town, it was obvious that the society that Zeke had known had changed.

The middle-class neighborhoods they toured looked destroyed, with broken windows and unkempt yards. What he saw reminded Zeke of conditions he had observed sometimes when he had travelled abroad for work to third world countries. He turned on the TV in the limo and saw news reports of riots, talks of an armed insurrection.

When that morning Zeke had watched the video that had been prepared for him, he had seen that things were politically chaotic during Trump's time in office. But now conditions appeared worse and the country less stable. Yes, in the past some young politicians had talked of an environmental Green Plan and raising taxes on the wealthy. Regular political stuff. They had talked about big oil and how it had to go away to save the planet. There had been talk of universal health under Clinton and another attempt by Obama and Biden, but it never came to full realization.

Other politicians called for the breakup of companies like Facebook and other tech companies, which were getting richer and more powerful than most countries. But these earlier efforts had been antitrust actions, not attempts to take over and "own" these companies and industries.

Zeke asked Peters to drive him to the local library. There he sat down and reviewed online the last ten years of this country in headlines and news reports. He saw that after the Trump and Biden Administration ended and Joan Wilkins was elected,

Wilkins proposed sweeping changes to help everyone in the country. But not much was implemented.

Then Bartlett took over after Wilkin's death. With the sympathy of the congress, he had gotten more of his proposals passed. Now unintended consequences were developing, which the country was mired in, with no easy way out. The road to hell is paved with good intentions.

Zeke came out of the library four hours later, stunned. What had we done to ourselves?

CHAPTER 8

# You Must Answer the Call

When Zeke got back to Mar-a-Lago with Peters, he was up to speed on this brave new world. There were still people who were in the top one percent of the extraordinarily rich in this new society. He guessed there always would be, in each society.

The new Federal Government was in the process of taking care of everyone. They just needed to get through this rough patch, they said. When the country emerged from this transition, everyone would be equal. There would be no discrimination or vast disparities of wealth and opportunities.

All would work at something the government would offer you, with a guaranteed wage and lifetime work, healthcare, and education. And peace would prevail throughout the land, they said. It sounded ideal, but what a mess was developing. The society was falling apart.

Zeke went to his room for about an hour to think. When Peters again knocked, they walked back through the lavish corridors to see the former president.

"Well, Zeke. It's hard to believe isn't it?" Mr. Trump said, shaking his head. "When I learned of your project from a friend at Waltham Scientific, I thought, 'What an amazing invention to help the world—a huge step forward.' You really struggled those first ten years. I kind of lost interest, but I was committed, and I stuck with you. As you started to uncover how to make a mature animal and accelerate and control their age at birth, your work got exciting again. But, like your wife Jane, I started to have second thoughts about it, about how easily people could corrupt your invention. After you were attacked by Coco, it was clear—we needed to destroy all of this. Then I had a brilliant thought: maybe Zeke can save our country."

"We must stop this growing anarchy, Zeke," he continued, "this unraveling of society.

"We need to find someone who can change history, turn things around. The election is just over one year away. Both parties are corrupt and not worth a damn. Jim Robinson and I have quietly started a new party. I have already done what is necessary to get the new Independent Party listed on the ballot in every state. There are a sizable number of politicians I trust who are ready to join the party—*if* we get a standard bearer they can get behind. We need a bigger-than-life leader, someone the people can see at a glance will lead them out of this mess. A lot like me, but not me. No more Trump. Beyond this work so far, I do not want to be involved. The country has had enough of Trump, even though many love me as the greatest president of all time. I will give you the money to run a slate of Independent candidates. Beyond that, we probably will not even meet again after today. This is all on you. Help fix America, Zeke."

With that Trump walked out, mentioning a golf game. What did the mogul expect the young scientist to do? Zeke retired again to his room, mulling over his options and all he had learned about the present political scene.

He had always been left of middle politically, but he could not believe how far-off course things had gone.

And because he, Zeke #2, had not been here in the crucial years, he could barely grasp how, why, or when this momentous societal and political shift had taken place and the country's problems had worsened.

Peters had told Zeke to feel free to summon him at any time, saying, "I'm at your service for as long as needed."

With a plan gradually taking shape in his mind, Zeke called Peters to his room. He explained that he needed to go back to the lab right away. Peters told him the jet would be ready in thirty minutes and, if he wanted, Peters would accompany him, to assist in any way possible.

He quietly informed Zeke that, as of today, "I no longer work for Mr. Trump. He dismissed me from his employ. He put two million dollars in my account as my retirement account, with his thanks. He said he felt I could be of more service to you and to

Jim Robinson, a person he holds in high regard." Peters told Zeke he would like to be part of the solution, knowing that Mr. Trump was trusting all three of them, this new little band, to take bold steps to save the country.

Peters gave Zeke a stack of forms—the official papers that had been filed to create a new political party. And a bank account statement showing a five-hundred-million-dollar balance, deposited there for the new party's use. Plans were getting serious fast.

Zeke and Peters were on the plane an hour and a half later, heading back to Logan Airport in Boston.

They barely spoke. Zeke was filled with questions about how to proceed. Zeke and Peters both loved America in a way that all Americans can understand. Whether one is a new immigrant of six months or a twelfth-generation American, it is a special place.

They both knew they had been given an extraordinary opportunity to try and save the country from itself, and the resources to proceed. But how? Zeke was not a politician. He'd rarely stuck his head up from his lab table before this. Did they know anyone in those circles of power who could help them?

As the plane glided into Logan, Zeke turned to Peters and said, "I think I know what I need to do, but I'm not sure I can pull this off. I am going to need some help. I need to know now, are you spying on me for Trump?"

Peters looked at Zeke. His eyes bore into Zeke's as he answered.

"I have no ties any longer with Mr. Trump. None. I am a free agent, and I want to help. This country allowed me to come from a single mother in poverty to where I am today. I want to help."

There was conviction and honesty in every word. Zeke knew he was set with a good partner and that Mr. Trump must have known it, too, to arrange matters in the way that he had.

The two men exited the plane, found their awaiting limo, and were driven directly to Zeke's lab. Using the keys, he'd been given earlier, Zeke swung open the big green steel lab door and flipped on the fluorescent lights that flickered to life. The place was spotless. No signs remained of the carnage that had occurred there only a few days ago.

A lifetime ago.

"In the documents, Trump gave me a list of names of people in the government who want to join the Independent Party of America, the new IPA," Zeke said. "Some are Democrats, some are Republicans. We must go to Washington or somewhere and essentially have a convention. At the convention, we will elect party leaders to run this party. We will also create a slate of candidates to run in the next election so that we can have representatives in Congress to help our legislation. We only have a year to get this work done before the next election. It's a tall task," Zeke concluded, handing the list back to Peters.

Peters took it and skimmed his eyes over it, his accumulated political savvy kicking in.

"These are some of the most powerful people in Congress," he said. "This is a good start. But we need a standard bearer. An unquestioned leader. Who among these politicians is that person?"

"Don't think he or she is on this list," Zeke answered. "But I have a good idea who it could be," Zeke said. He smiled at the audacity of what he was going to propose, keeping it to himself for now. "We need to reach out to all the people on this list. There are about two hundred members of the House of Representatives and amazingly forty senators. They are at present pretty much evenly split between the two current parties."

Peters suggested they get with Jim Robinson and start to call these politicians this afternoon. Peters and Zeke locked up the lab and went over to Robinson's house and discussed the plan and the seed money for the IPA.

Robinson was not surprised, and he knew from Trump that gears had been put in motion. As they made their calls, the response was overwhelming. A lot of groundwork had been done before today by Jim; the person Zeke had been known to this point as "our benefactor's messenger."

Zeke and Peters could only assume that Mr. Trump and Jim Robinson had been working on this giant, ambitious project for a while, laying the groundwork.

Many on the list said they disliked Mr. Trump personally, but that they would put the future good of the country over this dislike, as long as Trump was not involved past this point. They individually felt that their own parties had abandoned them with the current radical proposals.

The Republicans on the list felt their party did not do enough to resist this latest administration's proposals and were anxious to find a party that would give them the vehicle to change this situation once and for all.

The Democrats on the list were in many ways the most sensible people on the list. They were middle-ground people who had been unable to stop the popular swell of the far, far left after Wilkin's death.

Zeke had told Peters and Robinson to tell all the people called that the party's convention would be held in Charleston, South Carolina, in April of next year. He had them assure the people on the list that, in the meantime, an inspiring leader would be found and brought forward, to capture the imagination of America.

Zeke also suggested that Robinson and Peters begin to create the party's platform and develop the party's strategy for each state. They would need to hire staff across the country. The Senators and Representatives all knew Robinson well, and Zeke could see from the feedback that he got that Jim was highly thought of and respected.

After all he had built the party from the ground up.

Peters and Robinson knew that they would have to use this time between now and the convention to explain the new party to the American people. They would have to create some tentative planks for the party's platform now. To do that they decided to create a committee in secret, from the list of politicians, to begin that process. They would then put it out on social media and with the mainstream media. They wanted to accomplish these steps at least six months prior to the convention in Charleston. They got on the phone and secured the Charleston Convention Center and twenty thousand rooms for the four-day event. The deposits were just over two million dollars, which hardly put a dent in their war chest. Now came the hard part.

# CHAPTER 9

# It's Now or Never

While Malcom Peters scoured the Nashua area for office space to be the nerve center for the roughly four hundred staffers needed for the new Independent Party of America, Zeke decided to go on a road trip. He told Peters he would be back in about a week.

Other than that, he told Peters only to proceed with the interviewing and hiring of staff around the country. He assured Peters that he would tell more when he knew more. Before Zeke left town, he went to the local cemetery. He went to the rectory at the church where Jane was buried and asked the secretary where her grave was located. He found it in the far left of the cemetery near some Blue Spruce trees. He looked down at the stone, disbelieving. He ran his fingers over the chiseled letters in the granite, trying to feel her, touch her in some way. He sat on the ground with such a heavy heart and thought he might never get up again.

"Jane, where are you? Jane, I need you so much. I want you back with me.  Am I back with you now?" he wondered.  Finally, he slowly stood. "I am doing this for the right reason, Jane," he told her. "I have to believe you would understand."

Zeke started down Route 95 towards Boston. He wanted to go see his old professor at Harvard. Miles McDonald had taken Zeke #1 under his wing as a freshman some thirty years ago now. Miles had been a trusted advisor and became a lifelong friend. At the time, Miles had been a new teacher at Harvard, only twenty-seven years old. He too was very bright and had his first doctorate in physics at twenty-four years old. But gradually Miles had become more fascinated by history and political science. Though many mysteries still existed about the physical universe, Miles was, in the end, more drawn to study the mysteries of the political animal. He was now teaching political science classes and getting a second doctorate in the subject.

Miles had an engaging, good-natured disposition. He was now fifty-eight years old, athletic and wiry, about 5 feet 8 inches tall and 130 pounds. He loved playing sports of all kinds, especially basketball, where his quickness served him well and compensated for a lack of height. He was from Ohio, where his family had owned a five-thousand-acre dairy farm. His parents were strong, independent, and hardworking—the type of people sometimes referred to as forming the backbone of America. As prosperous as their farm was, the $79,000 a year Harvard price tag was too much for them. Luckily, Miles earned an academic scholarship to the school, which made his studies possible.

Miles and Zeke had remained close, despite the passing of the years and their divergent careers. Miles, of course, knew of Jane's passing and had been at the funeral. The friends had kept in touch afterwards, but Zeke had been more remote as his work in the lab intensified and even more quiet and distant after Jane's death. Miles had let it go, attributing Zeke's withdrawn mood to a preoccupation with research and to the effects of grief and mourning. So, Miles was happy to hear that Zeke was coming to visit. Zeke had not shared with Miles what his experiments were, only that they were top secret. Miles knew and trusted that someday he would learn what his friend had been working on so diligently all these years.

Now when Zeke called out of the blue, they agreed to meet at Harvard. Harvard Square had been converted to a pedestrian area a decade ago, so Zeke had to park in Alston and take the "T" to Harvard Square. Once getting off at Drake Street he walked about two blocks onto the Harvard Campus. Harvard Square was a mess. Papers littered the area, including the detritus from a rally--pamphlets supporting the changes in the country and others condemning it all. Several buildings were burnt out and boarded up, and the young students who milled around the square looked more like an angry mob instead of students out for a walk. Zeke entered the Roosevelt Building where Miles's office was and knocked on the door.

"Come in!" Miles shouted, and as Zeke entered the room, Miles let out a loud, "Hello, hello, you!" and jumped up, giving his friend a hug. "Hey, you look great—younger, so much younger. You look incredibly younger! I mean what are you doing, you look great. What brings you up out of your lab in the hills of New Hampshire?" Miles asked, smiling, after they had caught up for a while. He continued to stare at Zeke's youthful appearance, amazed.

"I wanted to see you to make me laugh," Zeke said, and part of that was true. "Well, I'll see what I can do about that!" Miles leaped up upon his desk in a single bound and posed like a muscle man on a beach, arms extended down across his body flexing. He still looked in good shape, a handsome guy, even as he was making fun of himself.

"I can't believe they still let you teach here. Haven't they found out you are too eccentric, yet?" Zeke said laughing. Miles bounded off the desk and landed in a Jimmy Durante pose, saying "A cha, cha, cha! No such thing!"

"No, seriously Zeke, why did you want to see me?" mimicking Groucho Marx shaking an imaginary cigar and moving his eyebrows up and down for effect.

"Enough already, stop," Zeke said. It was good to laugh. He had not done it since . . .. Boy, did he have a lot to tell Miles.

"Let's go to the faculty lounge across the way. We can get a drink and sit down and talk," Miles suggested.

"No, let's stay here for a while if you don't mind, Miles. I'd like to have some time to talk to you in a confidential setting."

"My, so serious," Miles said. "Sure, that's fine. I've got some soda here in this refrigerator if you would like some. We can sit here for as long as you like. I don't have another class until Thursday, two days from now. So, what's up?"

Where to start? Zeke had thought about this question all the way down to Boston. Much of what he had to tell was not too impressive or innovative from a scientific perspective. Taking a fertilized embryo and inserting a specific DNA was not all that earth shattering. But being able to replicate an animal and, for God's sake, himself—and at a certain age—these developments were mind bending. "What the heck had Zeke #1 got himself into?" he kept thinking with irritation. If he had never gone down this path, he would have had a lucrative lifelong position with Waltham Scientific or any research lab in the country. Reading that he got fired still blew his mind. Maybe Jane would have taken better care of herself, too, without the stress of Zeke's bumpy career to worry about. Maybe her husband would have noticed more about her health—paid closer attention—instead of having his head perpetually buried in that lab, as documented in those reports. On top of all that, the country was now falling apart, and somehow, unlikely as it seemed, he had become the person to try to save it, pull it together, and change the national destiny. It was going to be a difficult discussion for sure.

"Miles, what I am about to tell you is all true. It will be beyond anything you can reasonably believe as a scientist or political scientist. But it is all true. Don't stop me for questions. Let me finish, and then I will answer all the questions you have."

Zeke then went about telling him of being fired for wanting to do his own work with DNA. He explained how he set up his lab. About the anonymous donor and about the hundreds of failed experiments. When he got to the part about replicating an animal, Miles was not shocked. This type of cloning had been done in other labs, though not in an artificial womb. But he was not ready for Zeke's final claim.

"And I was able to recreate life at a certain time in a being's previous existence. To the day." Zeke went on to tell him about his dog Phoenix back at home, cared for by a neighbor, and all the markers he used to help determine the dog's age. Finally, he got to the experiment with Coco the chimp.

"So, I planned on seeing if I could replicate this work on a chimpanzee. Since the DNA of a chimp and a human is so close, this experiment was my next step."

Miles was getting uneasy at this point. He was suppressing a rage that was growing in him, at Zeke's hubris. Why did he think this work was needed in this world? With all the country's current problems, he thought he had seen it all. But this, fooling with God's work, made him sick.

"After starting the birthing chamber," Zeke continued with a returning sense of doom, "I let the process proceed for the number of hours and minutes needed to be successful. But this time, I returned to the lab—accidentally, inadvertently—past the allotted gestation time.

When I opened the birthing chamber, the animal inside the enclosure had become frightened and enraged. It leaped from the chamber and, and it . . . killed me. Before I died, I was able to subdue the animal and place my own DNA in the chamber and start the timing process. I must have made an error, as I was dying. I produced myself at thirty-two or thirty-three years old. That is who you have in front of you. The old Zeke is dead. I am his replica at thirty-three. I have had to read all his reports to learn what I had done. Otherwise, I would not know that I even owned a lab, since it had not even occurred to me as a possibility yet. Are you still with me?"

"Are you fucking shitting me? You expect me to believe this crap? I'm not the crazy one—you are." Miles rose to his feet red faced and angry. "You need help. If you really believe this story, I'm afraid for you." Miles went around his desk and stared out the window for a long time before turning to Zeke. He needed to cool down.

"I know you. You do look much younger than at your wife's funeral. The skiing accident you and I were on. It was your late thirties. I thought you would lose your leg. Let me see your leg.

Zeke raised his pant leg. He had had over two hundred stitches. There was nothing there. Miles stood staring at his leg. He violently lifted the other pant leg. Nothing.

"Zeke, what is going on? Is this true? Did you really do this, Zeke? This is horrible! Who are you?" Miles thrashed around the room violently trying to shake the grotesque image in his mind of Zeke recreating himself. "If this is true, you must destroy all of your notes. All your equipment. And never ever, speak of this again, to anyone." Miles felt sick to his stomach and ran to his adjoining bathroom, convulsively throwing up. He came back into his office after he had cleaned up. Zeke was still sitting in the same seat with his hands on his head, breathing heavily.

"I just didn't see the end game," Zeke said between gasps. "I was driven to do one thing, which I had thought would be beneficial, and I didn't see the ramifications. Or if I did, I did not want to see them. I've read that Jane had expressed concern about my work. She probably died begging me to stop. I don't know for sure because the Zeke in front of you wasn't even there!"

Hard as it was to believe, impossible as it was to believe, Miles thought maybe he did not have a mad scientist on his hands, or did he? Zeke looked so young, like the kid he knew in college. At around age fifty, Zeke had looked his age with some graying of his hair. He looked one hundred years old at Jane's funeral. This "kid" in front of him did indeed appear to be thirty something. Where was the scar? So, if this was Zeke, he had a man in front of him who was broken by some abominable success. Zeke was his dear friend, and slowly Miles's anger dissipated. It transformed instead into compassion for someone who was confused and needed forgiveness and help. Then, just as he started to convince himself the whole story may be true, Miles thought again it was all too preposterous to be believed, which meant his friend needed serious psychological help. Maybe it was the death of Jane that had pushed him into the deep end of the pool. Maybe he had had a skin graft to remove the skiing accident's scar and some amazing facial plastic surgery too. Miles turned and stared out his window over the courtyard at Harvard. The country was in shambles, his students were confused, angry, and lost, and his friend was nuts. He had a vision of life as he'd known it—now in shambles.

"Look, Zeke, this is a preposterous story. You can understand why I just cannot believe that much of it is true. I do not doubt you have cloned an animal. But that you are a clone?

And that you had discovered how to pick the age of a cloned creature? Please, it's too much."

"I know how this sounds. But I have been working on this research project for over twelve years. I have been financed for ten of those years by a generous anonymous investor. Who is Donald Trump.

"Okay, now Trump is in your story. That makes you certifiable. Trump barely got out of office in one piece. His harsh rhetoric, I feel, led to the election of Wilkins, which led to Bartlett, and now to the total meltdown of the financial and political structure of the U.S. These current actions by the government are almost an effort at a counterbalance of all he got passed by the Congress. But they went too far. Bartlett has gone too far."

"I didn't think you would believe me," Zeke said, composing himself. He felt steadier. "I want you to come to my lab. Right now. I'll show you this is all real."

"You want me to go to Nashua now. We will run into all kinds of traffic going North on 95. Come to my place tonight and spend the evening. We can talk more and then we will head out early tomorrow. We will be going against the traffic, and we will be in Nashua in less than an hour." Zeke didn't want to spend the night, but then he thought about being at his house alone. He didn't want that either.

"Okay, let's go downtown to Quincy Market and eat at the Marriott Long Wharf. They have a nice restaurant, and the view of the harbor is calming. And I need some calming." Miles said. Miles grabbed his fall coat and they headed out. It was a quick Uber ride over the Longfellow Bridge and through the Government Center to the Marriott. The area was almost empty with a few tourists. Boston had become a destination for many Europeans and Asians, and even in these strange times in the U.S. they still came. But the beautiful city of Boston was beginning to crack at the seams. Many of the store fronts were empty. Faneuil Hall still maintained its many businesses, but other than tourists no one went there. People didn't have the extra money to go out. If they had savings, they hid it under the mattress with fears this new Congress would somehow tax existing savings and impose a penalty that they would redistribute to the "people." Hell, they were the people, and everyone was scared. The people needed a savior.

Miles and Zeke went up the long escalator at the Marriott to the lobby and turned right to the restaurant. They got a table overlooking Boston Harbor. In better times, it would have been a night out.

"What can I get you, gentlemen?" the waiter asked. He was a man in his late fifties or early sixties.

"Kind of quiet here," Miles said.

"It's been like this for over a year now. Few people go out to dinner anymore, especially to a place like this. Tourists help, but we don't serve many Americans anymore. We are all too poor, including me."

It was a startling admission by a server who had been here in good times, so he could easily see and gauge these bad times. Zeke kept wondering, "Did the older Zeke know what was happening? Or was I—at that time--too out of it, too absorbed in my research project and my own concerns? Does social change happen so slowly that it is hard for busy individuals, caught in their own concerns, to notice and get alarmed about? What had Jane noticed about these changes in society and what had she made of them?" He'd never know. They gave the waiter their order. Fried clams and fries.

"Look, I believe that you believe your story, Zeke," Miles started off. "So, let's not challenge that. I will go to your lab in the morning, and that visit will settle it. Now let's just relax. Let's have a good dinner, a nice sleep in my apartment, which is only ten minutes from here, on Beacon Hill. Then we will put this matter to rest." Miles raised his glass of water and said, "To us, two incorrigible scientists who just want the truth."

"To us," Zeke replied. "May we have some better tomorrows."

The two old friends reminisced about the days they first met, since Zeke couldn't recall anything they did together after his early thirties. That blew Miles' mind. "I just don't remember," Zeke kept saying. "It doesn't exist in my mind." It was a good evening anyway. For a while Zeke forgot about his troubles and the immense obligations that he felt the future was requiring of him.

The next morning, they were both up and showered early. Last evening Zeke had gone out for a walk in the Beacon Hill area. It was still fashionable, but on every corner was a startling sight—a private security guard with a machine gun over his shoulder. Zeke was stopped several times and asked what he was doing in that neighborhood. Miles had given him a letter, saying he was an approved visitor. One of the guards called the number on the paper to check it out. Zeke finally decided just to go back to the apartment. It was depressing to be considered a suspicious character.

They pulled into the parking lot of the lab at 8:10 the next morning.

They had made good time from Boston, with most traffic tied up heading the other way into Boston, as Miles had foreseen. Zeke went over to the green steel lab door, unlocked it, and swung it open. He flipped a switch and the fluorescent lights flickered on. Miles was impressed by the lab. He quickly surveyed the machinery and saw the traditional equipment for the extraction of the DNA from a cell and an impressive storage area with DNA from worms to the opened and empty cylinder under humans. Other equipment he did not recognize.

These were the pieces that Zeke had painstakingly built over several years of trial and error. One looked like the Wilcott equipment Miles and Zeke were both familiar with. It had a large bin at the end of it—a rectangle space with a sign on it that said, "Birthing Chamber." It was large enough for a full-sized animal or person to fit in it. It was in this space that Zeke claimed he was able to replicate a mature animal—and himself.

"You can sit over there," Zeke said, as he pointed to Martha's chair, where she normally waited to receive her instructions and where she used to lay her coat or sweater. Zeke went over to the storage area and extracted a DNA vial from inside an ultra-low freezer set at -80C.

He then took a frozen embryo from another chamber. The thawing would begin immediately in another piece of Zeke's equipment, one that did the step more quickly and safely than many other commercial laboratories. In about thirty seconds, after Zeke had set all his equipment, he handed Miles a vial that contained the embryo and DNA samples, adjacent to each other but not yet joined.

"When I tell you to proceed, insert this embryo of a mouse and the DNA from a mouse in the equipment like so," Zeke explained, as he showed Miles the slot to insert the specimen.

"Well, the fertilized embryo of the mouse will be a mouse, Zeke. I don't understand why the DNA, too?" Miles asked.

"It's the DNA that I have learned to manipulate that produces the mature subject," Zeke said as he moved around his equipment, checking and adjusting dials and valves. Suddenly Zeke turned on the equipment, and the room was filled with the familiar low hum of energy activating powerful electronic equipment.

"Okay, Miles, insert the samples now," Zeke shouted over the din. Miles carefully slid the two samples into the birthing chamber.

"We now will have to wait 4 hours and 27 minutes to produce a two-year-old mouse," Zeke said with a smile. While they were waiting Zeke took Miles around the lab, explaining the equipment and especially the custom modifications. They then reviewed his notes that had been returned from Florida, which spanned years of trial and error and which carefully and in minute detail laid out what had been done to set the baseline for the test and the results of the test. Miles admired the determination of Zeke, but he was worried.

Zeke is going through these steps as if he thinks this will work. What happens when it doesn't work? Should he try to convince Zeke to commit himself for psychiatric observation? Then, what if what Zeke said was true? He had a sinking feeling in his stomach it was true. Then what? This discovery could be used in such diabolical ways. People with access could literally live forever. And what about this Zeke he is with now. What is he, a clone? How do you act with and treat a clone? He knows nothing of nearly the last twenty years of his life.

When four hours had passed the equipment automatically began to shut down. The low din decreased and finally there was silence, except for some scratching that was coming from inside the birthing room. Zeke opened a six-foot door on the top of the equipment, like a hatch on a bulkhead cellar door. And there it was. A fully grown mouse.

Miles was shocked. He reached down and grabbed the squealing mouse and examined it over and over. His mouth was agape all during his examination. Miles turned to Zeke and said, "Is this what you are? A replica like my friend here."

"I am Zeke, not a replica. Well, yes, I am a replica, but not some kind of model. I am the flesh and blood of Zeke. The mind of Zeke and the memories of Zeke, up until he was thirty-three years old. I've lost everything after that point, it does not exist in my world, until the moment I emerged from the birthing chamber, a few days ago."

Zeke was almost pleading with his old friend to understand and accept these unusual truths. Miles, however, was a scientist too and understood exactly what they were dealing with. And he was convinced he had to find a way to stop it.

Zeke said, "Let's leave the lab now. I want to take you to my house so we can talk. There is nothing else to see here."

"What about the mouse?" Miles asked, pointing at the little creature.

"I'll drop him off on my way home, at a farm near to my house," Zeke said. Before they pulled onto Reed Street, Zeke reached in the back seat and took out the box holding the mouse. "I hope you have learned how to outrun cats," Zeke said as he let the mouse scurry away into the weeds.

Miles's mind was racing, considering the good this invention could do and the bad. Could the good be used to lessen the heartbreaking tragedies that happened every day? Accidents, murders, childhood deaths from disease. No one had to lose anyone.

And when you get old, you could rebirth yourself as a young man or woman again. So, no one with money he expected, ever needed to die. How would this instant reincarnation work with nature? The world's population?

As they drove down the tree-lined street Zeke lived on. Everything was quiet and peaceful, but even here, Miles noticed with surprise, the yards were becoming derelict. There appeared to be cars broken down in many driveways and backyards, paint peeling, wood rotting, roofs sagging, and an air of abandonment. As they pulled into Zeke's driveway, he saw a dog in a doghouse in the fenced backyard.

The neighbors had been watching, walking, feeding, and loving Phoenix for Zeke.

"That dog I created about a little over a year ago now. His health is stable," Zeke reported in a monotone, scientific manner.

They walked through the little family room and sat down in the living room. Zeke poured Miles a glass of Cabernet. They both sat and stared at each other for a full minute before either one spoke. Even then, all Miles did was shift his weight and look around the room. Pictures of Jane and Zeke #1 were on the mantle, and some beautiful artwork Jane had bought many years ago adorned the walls. It was a beautiful home, just so empty without Jane.

They sat in silence. "You have to destroy your lab and all of your equipment," Miles finally said. "You must take all your notes and destroy them as well. No one other than the two of us can even know about this invention, and I guess Trump. What does he want from the deal? To live forever, God save me!"

"No, he apparently wants nothing. He supported this research when I was focused on the issue of food supply. I met with him recently, and he has left the matter of the lab in my hands, to do with what I want. He seems like a decent person." Zeke added. "But there is at least one other person who may know what I was doing—Trump's former right-hand man Malcolm Peters.

I don't know if they both viewed all that happened on a closed-circuit surveillance camera. As of now, I do not know if Peters knows everything or not. I didn't know if I knew the cameras existed at the time, but I learned of it now. The chimp attack and my death are even on tape. So, we can destroy the lab, but some people—those people—may know about it. I do trust Malcolm, though. He and I are now working together, and I believe in him."

"Trump, does he have some ulterior motive?" Miles asked again. "Has he made any demands of you? Can you trust *him*?"

Zeke was pleased. These questions meant that Miles had started to believe him, at least on the surface.

"As I told you, he is out. He realizes he cannot be involved in this business at all. As I say, his former assistant Malcolm Peters has left Trump's employ and now lives in Nashua, assisting me and another fellow in any way he can," Zeke explained.

"Assist you in destroying all the evidence, I hope."

"No, he is here for something bigger," Zeke said. He then shifted the topic to the one he had been thinking so much about. "Miles, you are a student of political science. You have studied our history, our current politics. Is it as bad as I think it is?"

"It is worse. When you start a system going down a road to change, it gets its own momentum. The current administration lied to the electorate. We thought we might be getting universal health care and some restrictions on polluting industries, but we got so much more—too much. As the Congress changed guidelines and laws to accomplish their promises, they needed more money. Taxes rose through the roof. Industries were being choked by regulations and started to flee the country.

"So, by Executive order restrictive laws were created on leaving the country that were found unconstitutional, but the damage had been done. The country is an awful mess. It has gone so far away from capitalism and towards socialism on all levels I do not think it can be changed or rescued. The people are angry. We are getting riots from soccer moms and black panthers and white supremacists all on the same side, under the banner of 'save our country."

Miles was now on his feet making a speech. It was an impassioned speech by someone who cared deeply and understood what has been done to our country's financial system and some of its laws.

"I have a solution," Zeke said standing up and facing Miles. He placed his hands on his shoulders and looked straight into his eyes. "They have formed, with the help of some other people, the Independent Party of America or the IPA. I have joined this effort. We have about 30 percent of the Senate and 40 percent of the House ready to leave their parties and join the IPA. We have filed papers in every state so that we can have candidates on the ballot on all levels of the State and Federal Government, up to and including the President. Our platform will take shape this summer, but it will be a capitalist's agenda and getting back to our Constitution, but with an understanding and an agenda to address the social needs and inequality that has always existed in this country.

The details of taxes and regulations will all be worked out in the convention. Now, we need a charismatic leader. One the people will flock to. A power speaker who can express our ideas and get the people to believe in our new party. And we have five hundred million dollars in our war chest to start."

Listening to Zeke, Miles's breath was taken away. The sweep of the vision was so vast, and the stakes so high. Even with the deep pockets Trump was providing, how could Zeke accomplish all these goals? And who could be the charismatic leader? It had to be someone else, someone powerful. Instantly Miles started to envision what was needed to save this country.

The money was there, the philosophy could be put in place. The power structure within congress was there. These were parts of a winning plan. But the people of the country had been double crossed by Bartlett. They trusted *no* political person. Then it hit him. "Are you thinking what I am thinking?"

"I am going to bring back Abraham Lincoln, George Washington, Franklin Roosevelt, and Lyndon Johnson," said Zeke. "They are going to lead our country out of this mess. Washington was a general, a war hero, and a person understanding the example he had to leave for future generations. Lincoln was a great politician, a war-time Commander and Chief, and a natural leader. Roosevelt and Johnson were the consummate politicians. Both had big ideas like the New Deal, Social Security, Civil Rights, and Medicare to appeal to most Americans. And then I will destroy my lab and notes."

"Are you crazy? This is unfathomable." Miles was at a loss for words, as his mind rolled over these thoughts.

The bringing back of famous people from the past was too incredible to believe, and it raised nothing but questions. First, should it even be done? If it were done, could these towering historical figures make any sense of today? And who would believe such a thing could occur anyway? Who will believe this "time-travel invention if it's even possible? And if it is possible, how will people from other centuries deal with the twenty-first century people and problems.

These people all carry baggage from their respective eras. Do they even want to be alive again? This whole thing is simply crazy. He did not believe it, and he's seen it with his own eyes. Another thought worried Miles. If Zeke could do this feat, another scientist would latch onto his accomplishment and try to replicate it. Even though it would probably be globally outlawed by all civilized nations, someone else would do it.

If news of the breakthrough gets out, about how these people were cloned, it could create a disaster, as people came to know of this extraordinary capability.

"If you bring these people back, what legal standing do they have?" Miles continued with his questions. "They are *dead*. Everyone knows they are dead. You would be in court for ten years fighting to give them legal status. Then what good would this be? You must abandon this whole idea and just destroy your lab. Be done with this and lead the IPA yourself." Miles was pacing back and forth as he wrestled with this outrageous situation. To think that yesterday he was in his office, smoking his pipe, and wondering how the political situation in the country would work out. Now he was as the center of it, enmeshed in bizarre "what ifs."

"I'm going to try this idea one person at a time. See how it works out. Who do you think we should start with?" Zeke was like a kid in a candy store. He was not going to hear any negativity. It was now or never.

# CHAPTER 10

# Miles Goes Above and Beyond the Call of Duty

Zeke and Miles headed back to Zeke's house.

Zeke called Peters and asked him to get some pizzas and meet them at his house. They had to make some big decisions. At this point Miles had gone from feeling he was in the twilight zone, to feeling back at least in the current dimension. He had been convinced the breakthrough was real and that a famous person could indeed be brought back. It could be done.

He started to think about it in a more positive frame of mind. What good could this advancement mean for the country? The idea of the IPA was a long time coming. For many years people have been frustrated with the two old parties. Parties have come and gone in our history before, so in the long view, this introduction of a third option was nothing new.

But could a third party exist and gain real traction? Could it win over members who wanted to belong to it? Would one of the existing parties morph into the IPA like the Whigs did with the Republican Party?

The time might be right.

Zeke pulled his car into the driveway. Automatically his heart leapt with happiness that he was home, home with Jane, and then just as quickly those feelings were dashed with the realization that she would not be greeting him. He slid out of the car and walked towards the front door. Suddenly he heard his name called out.

"Zeke, it's me, Jim Robinson. Do you remember me?" Jim asked. Zeke and Miles turned to see Jim walking up to the door.

"Of course, I do, Jim. Good to see you," Zeke said, shaking his hand and thinking, "Our benefactor's messenger." "What brings you by? Oh, by the way this is . . ."

"Miles Gordon of Harvard. Hello, Miles. How have you been?" Jim asked. Just then Peters pulled up with pizzas for everyone.

"Hey, Jim, how are you? I didn't know you were going to be here, or I would have gotten another pizza."

"Let's go inside, and I can share with you why I am here, fellas. I have a feeling this meeting has been planned by someone for a long time," Jim said, as they all headed into the house. Zeke saw that Jim and Miles knew each other, and Peters knew Jim as well, from a visit to Mar-a-Lago he was sure.

"I don't think we are all here by chance, gentlemen," Zeke said, as he led them into the living room. "Grab a seat. I'll get us all some sodas and beer." Zeke put everything on a tray from the kitchen and returned to a room, looking around with satisfaction at the team that had assembled.

"Let me start," Jim said. "For the last number of years, I have been working on forming the Independent Party of America or the IPA. My staff and I have spent five years establishing this new political party in every state of the union. Each state has its own rule on accomplishing this new political entity. The existing parties have made it almost impossible to accomplish, but the key word there is *almost*. We have also quietly been discussing what this party could be with many people in Congress.

"There have been some reports of our activities in the *New York Times* and *The Washington Post*, but for the most part we have been ignored as a bunch of whack jobs with no chance of doing anything of significance. Essentially, I am the de facto Party Leader, which you gentlemen can confirm or change. I have been in politics for much of my adult life. Primarily in the background. So, I am well known on Capitol Hill. About five years ago, as things started to deteriorate in the country, I was approached by a number of people who will remain confidential for now. They felt we needed a re-start for the country.

"They know I understood the inner workings of what needed to be done to accomplish creating a new political party. For five years I received funds to accomplish this task. We are now at this point of implementing this plan. Being in the background was always comfortable for me. But I was challenged by one of our supporters to take the leading role in this effort. I have found that this is where I should be.

"So, I would like to remain the IPA's party leader. I am also considering running for office. I have been told to do so I would have to be vetted and approved but our yet unknown leader.

"I understand Zeke has been working on getting us a leader to bring this whole party together. So now I guess you have the floor, Zeke."

Zeke stared hard and long at Jim Robinson as everyone in the room did, too. Jim was an impressive and impassioned speaker. Dark skinned, black hair, a face and chin chiseled out of granite, and a smile that could light up the room. Everyone present had the same thought: this *is* the guy we need to be the IPA Party Chairman. "It seems we are all part of a plan," Zeke finally said. "A good plan, I think. But Miles, you were seen by me as a happenstance. I'm not sure if you knew you were going on this ride or if you even wanted to."

"Zeke, I have been watching the political landscape of our country in the past five- or six-years morph into something I don't recognize. It started out with the promise to create a society of fairness and equality for all. Making large corporations pay their fair share and taking care of our environment. A place where health care was a given for all our citizens. But what it has done is create a society of the haves and the have-nots. There is no one in the middle, where most Americans used to reside. We need a party that the Democrats had when JFK was elected. One that was more caring about the poor and disadvantaged, and that respected our constitutional values as well, and capitalism. Hell yes, I am all in." Miles slapped his hand on the coffee table to emphasize his point. "I will take a sabbatical from Harvard."

"Ok, here we are," Zeke said, "the IPA party. We need an unquestioned leader to inspire the average citizen. Someone people will instinctively recognize as a leader and who will want to follow the ideals of the IPA platform. I've thought a lot about this, and I think we should nominate George Washington," Jim said, jumping to his feet, "Sure, that would be great, but he's been dead for 230 years give or take. Unless you mean that metaphorically!"

"No," Zeke said, "I mean the real George Washington."

"Okay, I'm out," Jim said, as he threw up his arms in disgust. "This is serious. I have spent the last five years dreaming of this party and treating it like a baby. I cannot be in a group of nut jobs. I'll take this whole party with me now and leave." Jim started for the door in disgust, as Zeke yelled out to him.

"Jim, would someone of Washington's character interest you? Someone who it is historically stated that you knew was 'the man' the minute he walked into the room. Someone who was a bit understated, even quiet. But who, when he spoke, everyone had to listen? Also, someone who respected the words that shape our constitution. Would you like someone in the contemporary world who could be that person?"

"Of course, I would, Zeke. Do you know someone who fits that bill? I know all the politicians on Capitol Hill, and while we have many good men and women up there, no one I can think of meets all those criteria."

"Okay, Jim, Peters, and Miles," Zeke pleaded. "Will you give me a chance to present to you all someone who I think will be right in all those ways? Someone whom you know can bring this party alive for the average person. Jim, would you give me a chance to bring the person forward for your evaluation?"

"Sure, I would," Jim said. "I thought you meant the real George Washington, the way you first said it. I understand the type of solid character you are speaking of. And I would be glad to have this man come before us and let us meet him. Make an evaluation. Excuse my abruptness, but you did sound crazy there for a minute."

"It's okay. I understand, Jim. I am a scientist, not an articulate speaker such as yourself. I will need about six months to put this meeting together with this gentleman. At that time, I will arrange a meeting with this person I have in mind, and we can all make a decision together if this person is the right person for our new party."

Zeke realized that only Miles had any idea of what he was talking about. Peters didn't seem to know what Zeke was talking about, so that was good. The only person who knew was Miles, Trump, and . . . Zeke #1's assistant? Zeke #2 had never met this person. How much did she know about the research she was helping with?

"Martha," Zeke, thought to himself with a jolt. "I need to see Martha, as quickly as possible."

The men spent the next five hours creating an outline of the type of platform the IPA would stand on. These were men of good will and similar ideas. Some were more conservative than others, but in the true meaning of politics at its best, they sought out middle ground. At the end of the evening all departed, except Miles.

""You're not going to tell them, are you?" Miles said.

"How can I, Miles? Did you see Jim's reaction without knowing what I was really talking about? If he reacted that way, how do you think the public in general would react? They would think of this person, or me, as a cyborg or some sophisticated computer robot. The general public will never be able to wrap their head around this . . . revived . . . person being legit. It is going to have to be a secret between you and me. Is that something you are willing to sign on for?"

"You seem pretty normal to me, so yeah. I love this country too much not to try a daring fix, even something as radical as this. How did you settle on Washington?"

"Putting aside each person's politics, of the men I listed—Lincoln, FDR, and LBJ—they are too recognizable. Everyone knows about Lincoln, and his pictures and statues are everywhere. Same with FDR and LBJ. They are too contemporary and recognizable. Too many pictures and newsreels about them. George Washington could be the least recognizable. He is often pictured with puffy lips from the ivory and slaves' teeth he had fashioned as false teeth. And how many pictures have you seen of him without his wig? There is his history with slavery. That we will have to address. It could be a problem."

"There are some paintings of him as a young man without a wig, but that is about it. I just think we can pass him off as just another guy. That is why I finally picked him. Plus, in his time, he knew how to set the tone for future generations. That is what we must do now. Find someone to set a new tone for the IPA party and the country."

"Do you really think an eighteenth-century man can function in the twenty-first century? I mean we have eighty-year-olds now who do not carry cell phones. It seems a stretch to me," Miles said as he sat back down on the sofa.

"The way I see it, we isolate him at first. Gradually reveal him to where he is and what we have done. As impossible as it seemed to Jim and as outrageous, I think someone from two hundred years ago could swallow this coming back easier than Jim did. We don't need him to necessarily carry the entire burden of this venture. We just need him to give the party a coalescing figure who rallies people together and provides a kick start. But getting down to logistics, where to get the DNA?"

"Well, Washington is buried at Mount Vernon. He spent his last year at Mount Vernon. He died at Mount Vernon. I guess we could start there. Where else better to get some DNA? There are also uniforms he wore in the Smithsonian and other museums in and around Washington. Just iffy on finding DNA on cleaned material. This crucial step may be the most difficult part of the whole effort. Getting his DNA," Miles said.

The two men talked and planned for another two hours and then retired for the evening, with Miles going back to work at Harvard the next day to teach his class. Zeke felt he needed to see Martha before he did anything else. He called her and asked her to meet him at the lab. She refused, saying she would have trouble returning there, after what she had seen. But she was interested in how Zeke was doing—was he okay?

He assured her that he was fine, and she invited him over to meet her at her house that afternoon. She gave him the address on Day Avenue. As he drove through Nashua on his way there, he observed an unusual number of people outside, on the streets, and in the neighborhoods. He assumed they were looking for work. He was trying to notice more about the real world now that he was out of the lab.

He turned toward the town's main drag and then down Day Avenue.

It was a nice street of mostly Victorian style homes, ornate and elaborate. Martha's house was a large white Victorian home with light blue trim, neat and pretty. Zeke pulled into the driveway and sat for a minute. What was he going to say to Martha? What was she going to say to him? She knew him well, from years of working together, but this Zeke had never actually met Martha before. Well, he thought, here goes nothing.

He slid out of his car and walked up to the front door. The doorbell had a deep chiming of a Winchester Cathedral tune. In another minute, there was Martha, smiling and welcoming him. Was it Martha? He guessed it was!

"Dr. Leonard, please come in. I am so pleased that you are all in one piece. The last time I saw you, you were in several pieces," she said, as she walked them to her sitting room. Zeke didn't know what Martha did or didn't know. He only knew of her only from the report he read on the plane. Those notes had stressed her recurring role in operating the equipment. He knew that he needed to cover his bases in talking with her, but what bases? Now it was cat-and-mouse questioning time.

As they settled down into comfortable facing chairs, Martha took a deep breath and said, "I thought you were dead the last time I saw you. In fact, I'm fairly sure you were dead. But here you are.

"This is all a bit much for me to grasp. But I was your assistant, Dr. Leonard. I knew in general what you were working on. I just never knew how far the research and experimentation could all go." Martha was now looking straight into Zeke's eyes, somewhat like a teacher chastising a mischievous child.

"Martha, can you tell me what you know? Were you in the lab during the accident?" Zeke asked.

"Yes, after it was completed. I knew you were in bad shape. That is all I know." Zeke had the feeling that Martha had been coached, but how far should he push this?

Martha suddenly volunteered, "I signed an NDA the day I went to work with you, Dr. Leonard. I have no option but to honor that document. I will not end my life being a dishonorable person. I have lived by a strict moral code all my life, and I will not be changing that now. But what is this all about, Dr. Leonard? I took the embryo and DNA out of your hand and placed it in the birthing chamber, as I have a hundred times before. You were on the floor dying, alongside what I think was a dead chimpanzee.

"Blood was everywhere. I had to throw away all my ruined, bloodstained clothes and shoes when I got home. It was awful. And now here you are, alive and looking younger than I have ever seen you. I thought you were dead but look at you. And not a scar. Totally healed. When I was leaving to call 911, a black van pulled up and four men dressed in white operating gear jumped out. They told me they were there to save you. Not to worry and go home. And they would be in touch with me. They called me two days later and said you were recovering in a private hospital. When I asked if I could come and see you, they said no. That you were having extensive experimental plastic surgery and not having visitors.

"They said they were creating new parts for you in your birthing chamber. Putting you back together, piece by piece is what I was told. It looks to me that your experiment has been a total success." Martha had just followed her script perfectly.

In his research logbook, Zeke had noted many times that he had asked Martha to leave, prior to the end of the experiment. So, he thought, she really had no direct knowledge of his lab's capabilities and his end game. Maybe he could use that fact to his advantage.

"I never expected that I would be the subject of my work, Martha. From those samples I can create an eye, an ear, or whatever is needed from the person's own DNA. Since it is from the person there is no rejection of the parts that are needed. The surgeons barely saved my life. I had lost a lot of blood, but they were prepared with everything to save me."

Zeke hated to lie to Martha, but for the greater good he felt he had to limit the people who really knew what he was doing. Secrets tend to leak in politics. The fewer people who knew that the lab could produce living people who had been dead, the better. If she knew that capability, and suddenly saw a guy with Zeke who looked like Washington, she could maybe put two and two together. He fully expected to destroy everything one day and tell her all. She deserved to know. But until then he wanted just three people to know about the lab's capability: Trump, Miles, and him. He was pretty sure that Peters was in the dark.

"My benefactor had cameras hidden in the lab, Martha. His team saw everything that happened.

"I had brought in the chimp to create a new internal organ for the beast as he was dying of a failed liver. I planned on doing the surgery in the lab, but for some reason the ape attacked me. He tore into me bad. It must have been awful for you, Martha. I thought I put the samples of my ears in the birthing chamber. Now I realize you did.

"After they stabilized me other parts were created for me as I went through surgery after surgery. My benefactor has trained his people to do this for me. But we must keep this a secret for now. Even though this process has worked for me, my benefactor wants more work done before we release my findings to the medical community."

His story was far more believable than that he was a whole new being sitting before her. Growing replacement parts was not a new idea, and many researchers had worked for years on making it a reality. So, it was something that Martha could believe, he hoped. Zeke finally relaxed, having hit upon a semi-plausible story.

"I am so relieved. I really thought I saw you die. It was awful. But thank God you are alive."

And with that statement Martha let him off the hook. The conversation worked out just as they had planned it would, Martha thought. She reached across the coffee table and took up Zeke's hand. Everything was going to be fine.

Zeke sat with Martha for well over an hour, getting to know her all over again. She was the perfect assistant for him. He could see why he had chosen her. Bright but with a discreet lack of curiosity. She told him again that she was reluctant to go back to the lab.

The memories were just too traumatic. Zeke accepted her indirect resignation and thanked her for her loyal help all these years. After leaving, he arranged to have a fifty-thousand-dollar bonus sent to her, in appreciation for her work. Even though he was convinced of her promise to keep their work quiet and confidential between them, a little bribe never hurt. And she had been a good assistant, always coming and going at just the right times.

The following day Zeke drove to Boston to pick up Miles.

Miles and Zeke travelled together to Mount Vernon, outside of Washington, D.C. It took them five hours to get to the famous homestead of George Washington. Miles had gone over as much information about the national museum as he could find. Many articles in the house were George Washington's, but their best bet of obtaining a DNA sample was from his crypt, which is perhaps one the nation's most revered historical locations.

As they parked their car in the sprawling visitor lot, they noticed off to the side several signs pointing towards Washington's resting place. They walked over with a group of tourists. A small open building arched over the above-ground tombs of George and Martha Washington.

A guide was giving a talk on Washington's place in American history. As he was speaking, Zeke noticed another burial plot. He walked over to read the marker on the ground, which indicated where the graves of slaves who had died on Washington's plantation were laid. It was a common grave holding over 150 souls, unmarked except for this one tablet. It held the remains of people who lived from birth to death in slavery, owned by our nation's first Commander and Chief and his wife.

Zeke made a note to himself to learn more about this subject, before his new Washington arrived.

Miles had been reading up on what their challenge was going to be.

"Zeke," he said, "Washington's tomb is on the right. Martha's is on the left. The casket is lead lined with a mahogany exterior. It was moved here several years after he had been buried. At the time it had deteriorated. You never know what's going to be inside. I hope it is something that we can use, but there are no guarantees. In digs, DNA has been found that is thousands of years old and still viable, but only if conditions were exactly right to preserve the cells for DNA extraction. Often what worked well was being encased in a glacier that was melting."

"We have to come back tonight," Zeke whispered. "I imagine there will be guards, but we will have to measure the risk when we see what we are facing," he continued. "Let's go inside the house and see if any other potential source crops up."

As they entered Washington's home, Zeke asked an attendant, "Is there a manager on the grounds today?"

"You mean my boss? Yes, she is here. Is there a problem, sir?"

"No, but could I see her, please?", as Zeke handed him his business card.

"Let me go see if she has time for an unscheduled appointment. I will be right back." With that the attendant was gone. In about five minutes he returned. "Ms. Zola can see you now," the attendant said.

Zeke and Miles were led to a small building outside of the mansion. They entered a beautifully appointed office with two American Flags framing an ornate desk. Sitting behind her desk was a neatly coiffed and attractive lady, who stood to greet her guests with a warm handshake. She was close to six feet tall, with brown skin and bright, friendly eyes.

Ms. Zola was a brilliant statistician and historian who had been with the Federal government for many years. She was a highly respected and valued member of the many administrations she worked for while at the Pentagon, and she exuded a friendly but brisk and no-nonsense air of authority.

"What can I do for you gentlemen?" Ms. Zola asked.

"Let me introduce myself," Zeke said. "My name is Dr. Zeke Leonard, and this is my colleague Dr. Miles McDonald of Harvard University. We are working on a DNA project funded by the University where we are extracting DNA samples of people such as former presidents to record and keep preserved for future study. While much work is being done with DNA in the medical fields, we think that collecting and cataloging these samples may someday be of value to society.

"As we learn more and more about the human genome, who knows where this storage data bank could lead. That is the reason we have travelled here."

"Oh, that sounds fascinating and how are you Dr. McDonald? I have attended several of your presentations in Washington on the politics of today. They were fascinating and I must say, if I don't embarrass you, you are a very handsome man," Miss Zola said with a warm smile. "But gentlemen any work like that has to be approved at the highest levels at the Mount Vernon Ladies' Association. I have to receive authorization from them to work on any project such as what you have described." Ms. Zola explained in a firm but apologetic way.

"We sent along that request over one year ago. When we kept calling, they finally told us we have been approved and to see the manager of record at Mount Vernon to see what we can accomplish." As he explained his predicament, Zeke made his expression into one of sorrow mixed with exasperation. "We would not be intrusive. We would be out of here in no time."

"I don't know. I've not received any letter of authorization. Still, I am uneasy having you do anything without official, signed approval from the Association. You will have to come back later, with the proper paperwork."

Ms. Zola was a good manager. She had been in government service at the Pentagon for over twenty years. She knew exactly how the system worked.

"We have driven down today thinking all these clearance matters had been addressed, Ms. Zola. Is there anything you can do to help us? We don't know if we can find a cell from which we can get a DNA sample that has not deteriorated. We just need a small scraping from something personal of the President, something he was in contact on a regular basis. We would not damage the item. Would you please help us?"

Her usual work interactions involved helping sick tourists or dealing with people who tried to get past the roped off areas of the mansion. This inquiry was the most interesting one that Ms. Zola had had in some time. Plus, these two men from Boston looked reputable, and they did have good credentials, especially the professor from Harvard.

"Well, I might be able to do something," Ms. Zola said. "There are a number of articles that are not shown to the public. As you may know, President Washington was bled extensively when he became ill and was dying. He was still a robust man and probably had a simple throat infection that took his life. This bleeding, done by Dr. James Crack, left several blood stains on the bedding of the President's bed. These articles were never touched after his death and have been preserved as relics. They now reside in vacuum glass sealed containers away from the public. If there is anything of him left in existence, it might be there.

"If I show you that material, I need you, Dr. McDonald, to come with me to make sure we maintain privacy, while Dr. Leonard looks at this material. You cannot under any circumstances cut the material, do you understand, Dr. Leonard?"

"Yes, of course. We understand your guidelines." Zeke said, surprised that she was agreeing to allow them even to see these articles, never mind trying to get some DNA samples from them. It appeared to Zeke she was pretty attracted to Miles.

"Good, follow me."

As Ms. Zola led them from the room, she took Miles's hand and said, "You stay with me. I have a place where we can keep an eye on things."

She not only grabbed his hand but made sure her body lightly brushed up against his. Miles has been around women in his graduate classes who tried to come on to him over the years. He was single, athletic, and very handsome. He wasn't unfamiliar with this overt flirting. He always kept his professional distance, but it seemed to him this time, to accomplish their task of national importance, he might have to rewrite his own rules. He had seen this look many times before.

They were led to the back of the mansion where there was an entrance to the basement level under the home. This area was of modern construction.

Apparently, some or all of the foundation of the house had been replaced. In this basement area were rooms lined up on either side of a long hallway. It was nicely lit. Ms. Zola led the men to the third room on the right. She opened a lead door and flicked on a fluorescent light. There were several items under different glass enclosures. They appeared to be sealed. Ms. Zola approached one with folded sheets neatly stacked under the enclosed case. She pushed a button, and the case slowly lifted with a "whooshing" sound as the vacuum was released.

One end of the enclosure allowed the sheet to be observed at a close proximity.

"Please be careful. Occasionally these sealed cases are opened for different reasons, but we try to limit their exposure to the atmosphere. It will automatically seal itself when we are finished and then will extract the air in the container. Miles, you need to come with me while Dr. Leonard gets to work."

Miles let Ms. Zola lead him from the room, looking over his shoulder at Zeke with the look of a sheep going to slaughter. "Keep her busy," Zeke mouthed to Miles as he left the room.

Zeke examined the sheet, and he could clearly see the blood strains over two hundred years after they had occurred. He took out of his case a test tube and a sharp scalpel.

He gently lifted the sheet and put his finger under the largest stain he could see without removing the sheet altogether from the enclosure. With the scalpel he scrapped the stain where he found a lump of congealed matter. There was material on the blade that he could see. He still placed the scalpel in the tube and sealed it. Zeke carefully folded the sheet back into the case. He pushed the button next to the glass covering.

The glass top slowly descended and sealed the sheet. He could hear a subtle vacuum sound as the air was taken from the case. He removed his gloves and packed up his bag. Zeke used the same PCR laboratory technique used in other labs to recover even the most minute traces of the genetic code.

Now he had to find Miles.

As he walked out into the hall, Miles and Ms. Zola were emerging from another side room, pleasantly chatting. with Ms. Zola, and Ms. Zola had her arm around Miles.

"Did you get what you needed, Dr. Leonard? I hope we all got what we needed." She said with a smile and led the men out of the basement still holding onto Miles, into the sunlight of a beautiful fall day.

"Thank you, Ms. Zola, for your assistance. We will be leaving now. Zeke shook her hand. As he did, she turned to Miles and said, "You have my number. Please give me a call when you are in D.C. again, will you Dr. McDonald?" And with that, the two men turned and headed for the parking lot.

"What happened there?" Zeke asked.

"You could say we got to know each other a bit," Miles said, shaking his head. "I am constantly amazed at the effect I have on women."

They left to begin their five- to six-hour trip to New Hampshire. All Miles would add about his encounter was, "I only regret that I have but one body to give to my country," and that was it.

Back in the laboratory Zeke immediately took his samples to the equipment he had used to extract DNA samples from cells. All he could hope is that among the samples that he had taken he could find what he needed.

He worked on these samples for eight hours, carefully reviewing the results of each effort. When he emerged from the lab, he had what he needed: a cell, containing what he fervently hoped was George Washington's DNA, from more than two hundred years ago.

Immediately upon this success, he started the next step of his project. They had spent a lot of time preparing.

While they were gone, they had given Peters a list of items they needed for a bedroom. Peters had then set up the room in minute detail provided to him by Miles. Once Miles had seen the room in person, he texted Peters the subtle changes that he needed made. Peters had no idea why he was doing this, but he scoured antique shops in Boston and found much of what was needed without question and concern of the cost. He finished the room while Zeke and Miles were in the lab working on something that Peters did not have a clue about.

As he reviewed the appearance of the room with candlelight, he was pleased that all seemed to be as requested. Having worked for Trump for many years, he was used to completing tasks without question. The room was furnished with eighteenth-century furniture and was close to an exact replica of Washington's bedroom at Mount Vernon. Electrical outlets were sheet rocked over, taped, and painted. Nothing was in the room that spoke of either the nineteenth, twentieth, or twenty-first centuries.

In the lab Miles took over the duties of assistant, standing in for Martha. Zeke had instructed him on his role. They had discussed what they should do upon the emergence of George Washington from the birthing chamber.

He would be naked, and he would not know he had died. He will think he is back in 1796, the year Zeke decided to bring him back. He would still be President. Everything would seem out of whack. It could put him in shock or worse. They decided that when the birthing was complete Zeke would immediately administer a sedative. They would then dress him in undergarments and a nightgown like what men of that age would wear. They would transport him sedated to Zeke's house.

The room Peters had replicated was ready. Now to bring George back into this world. Zeke and Miles got the equipment operating. The DNA sample and fertilized embryo were ready to be inserted into the birthing chamber. They looked at each other and Zeke said, "I've decided this will be the last time this equipment will be used. If this doesn't work so be it. I have decided there will be no further sacrifices of our unique humanity.

"May God have mercy on us."

CHAPTER 11

# Exactly How Fast Are We Going?

Once they had inserted the embryo and DNA and started the equipment they left and went to a little pub he remembered Jane and he would frequent the Town Talk. As they entered, Wendy greeted Zeke with a big smile and a hug.

"Dr. Leonard. It is good to see you. How are you doing?"

Zeke was taken back but quickly caught himself. She was on the jet with him, so she probably has some tie with Trump, he figured. Why else would she be here, too? And since this was his and Jane's regular pub, he probably knew her from in here, but he could not go any further than the trip down on the jet.

"Much better. You were extremely helpful. Thanks. Have you seen Jim Robinson?"

"No, not since the trip back to Logan. Would you like your regular?" Wendy asked.

"Sure. Ah, this is Miles," Zeke said.

"Hi Miles, I'm Wendy. What can I get you?"

"I'll just have a glass of your house cab. Let's sit over here, Zeke. It looks quiet," Miles said.

As they sat down in a corner booth Zeke whispered to Miles, "I've probably known her for a long time. I assume I came in here with Jane and since her passing, too. So, we are probably on normal talking terms. Somehow, I feel close to her though. Like we had a friendly connection. But I have no way of knowing this. She was on the plane to Florida to see Trump. It is too much of a coincidence. I have learned that I have been watched closely over the past eleven or twelve years. Especially in my lab. I think everything was taped and reviewed by him or his people. He probably knew I came in here, and he probably had Wendy put here to keep tabs on me and Jane, I guess. I am learning no one gives away fifteen million dollars without some control and subtle supervision. Pretty thorough guy."

Wendy came over with Miles's drink. "You are looking so much younger. Like twenty or twenty-five years younger. I was shocked when I saw you on the plane to Florida. It looks like we are the same age now! I won't say any more about that trip. I'm sorry I brought it up."

"It's okay, Wendy. Do you work for Trump, too?"

"Well, yes I do, Zeke. I have worked on his jet periodically over the past 4 or 5 years since he bought this place. Whenever his people call, I make arrangements to steward his flights."

"Has he asked you about me?" Zeke inquired. "Oh yes, sure. He told me you worked for him and he wanted to know if you were all right. I always told him you were really happy, especially when Jane was with you."

"Miles here is working with me. What did you know on that trip?"

"I can only tell you this. I was told you had had a stroke or something and were unconscious. They were taking you to specialists in Florida. You woke up so confused. And then you seemed to be shocked with what you were reading. I guess the shock made you forget about the passing of Jane. That was just so sad and awful, Doctor. We had spent many hours talking since Jane passed, and you were right back at the beginning. My heart just broke for you. I cried in the jet all the way home." Wendy said, tearing up again. She wiped away the evidence.

"Yes, I needed help. And I got it in Florida—thanks for your concern. I still do not remember much about the last year. Must have been the results of a type of stroke," Zeke said.

"Well, when you have time, I'll fill you in, okay? You look good, though, I have got to say. You look so much younger. What's your secret?"

"Believe me, it's not worth it. How old are you anyway?" Zeke asked.

"I'm twenty-nine years old, Zeke. I am thinking of getting my doctorate, but I think I'm getting too old. Plus, I do like the job

I have now. I have a great employer," she said with a wink as she left the table.

"Jim Robinson, Peters, Wendy—they are all tied to Trump," Miles said. "You can bet on it."

"But why? I was not working on this particular project, or at least where it ended up. Jim is clearly a separate project. Peters came on later to help me after Florida. Wendy maybe is just a touchstone for him. Just someone on the periphery of Jane and my life who kept Trump up to speed on us. Who knows? She's probably already told me, and I don't know it anymore," Zeke thought aloud.

The two men ordered dinner and planned for Washington's arrival. It was not going to be easy and they knew it. They were taking a huge risk. Could he adapt? Would he cooperate? They only knew him from the history books, biographies, and his writings. They also needed to immerse him in today's English. If he was going to speak for the Independent Party and get it going, he had to talk in twenty-first century English.

They felt confident they could change his appearance to look modern, but the speech remained a question.

"I think once he understands why he is here, his sense of duty to the country will drive him to help. At least I hope that is what happens. And I hope he does not die again from a stroke, from the shock from what we have done to him," Miles said.

They finished up dinner at the pub and headed to Zeke's lab and bed. As they headed out the door Wendy said to Zeke, "You take care of yourself. If you need me to make you guys some dinner tomorrow night, I am off. I'd be glad to help."

"We are going to be tied up, Wendy, but thanks for the offer. I'll take a rain-check," Zeke said.

As they walked to the car Miles said, "I think you guys are friends, Zeke, don't you?

"I guess!" Zeke said, a little surprised. He used to be so much older than her. But now their ages were similar, and he felt a closer connection. They stopped at the lab, checked the equipment and then headed to Zeke's home for bed and the long wait. They were nervous with anticipation and neither slept well that night.

They spent the next day in the lab waiting. Miles reading history about Washington on his lap-top and Zeke checking and rechecking his equipment.

Just twenty-five hours and fourteen minutes later, Zeke and Miles heard the equipment suddenly become silent. Then some movement inside the birthing chamber. They quickly opened the door. There was a man, a man who looked like George Washington, the very man, himself, in person. Before Washington could utter a word or even focus on where he was, Zeke injected him with a sedative, and the former President was unconscious. Zeke and Miles stood there looking, and then looking some more, at President George Washington. *President* Washington . . . in the flesh. They felt stunned by the appearance of this historical figure.

They and all Americans had studied him since grade school.

In person, he was a muscular man with broad shoulders, built like a linebacker. They saw he had large feet, size 13, it turned out. He was tall—6 feet 2 inches in stature. They noticed he had high cheekbones, a long straight nose, and brown hair. He obviously powdered his hair for many of his portraits, a common practice in those days. His mouth was somewhat sunken, as he had no teeth. He looked all his sixty-five years and more. He had spent eight years as the Commander of the troops, eight years as leader of the Continental Congress, and, at that point, a little under four years as President. Who wouldn't look old?

Zeke and Miles carefully lifted this big man from the birthing chamber onto a gurney. He must weigh about 200 pounds, Zeke thought. They carefully dressed him in the sleeping garments of his day, which they had gathered ahead of time. They wheeled the gurney out to a waiting van they had rented. The gurney had collapsible legs, and they pushed it right into the back of the van. Zeke was struck by the emotions he was feeling. He was in the presence of perhaps the greatest man in American history, one of the greatest in world history, and it overwhelmed him.

The import of what they were doing was not lost on Miles either. A student of American history and politics, he too was awestruck by this man's presence in front of him. It was an emotion that they had not expected.

"Oh my God, Zeke. What have we done?" Miles turned to Zeke after they closed the door to the van, holding back tears. "What have we done? I can't believe this is happening. It feels . . . momentous."

Zeke went over to Miles and put his arm around his friend. He too had tears in his eyes. "Please, God, guide us in this . . . this effort to save America. Let's get him to bed." They both stumbled into the van and rode over to Zeke's house.

On the way home, they barely spoke, lost in their own thoughts. It is one thing to imagine meeting someone like this, someone who transcended myth. It was another thing to physically be in his presence. To touch him. To see him draw a breath.

As they pulled into the driveway, they carefully opened the van door. Washington was still sedated and would be for a short time longer. They pulled out the gurney, and its legs folded out onto the ground. They wheeled him up the walk and were opening the door when the mailman walked up Zeke's drive.

"Hey, Dr. Leonard. Got some mail for ya' here. What'cha got there?"

"Oh, it's one of my experiments," Zeke said, as he casually pulled the sheet over Washington's head.

"I didn't know you worked with bodies. Is that person dead?" the mailman asked as he poked around the gurney.

"No, no, he's just sedated. I didn't want to stay in the lab while he was asleep. It's easier for me over here," Zeke said, as he and Miles rolled the gurney into the house.

"Ok. I just hope I don't read about ya' in the paper tomorrow," the mailman said with a laugh. Zeke and Miles laughed along with him.

Finally, they got inside and shut the front door. They took Washington into the bedroom that Peters had put together and were amazed by the set up. The carpets, hardwood floor, wall coverings, furniture were all just as in Washington's bedroom at Mount Vernon.

"We have to stabilize him and let the sedation wear off. He only has a small dose so he will wake shortly. I have garments for us to wear to enter his room. They are styles from that time frame. We must introduce him to what has happened carefully. Let him wake thinking he is waking with a new doctor called in to help him.

He's the President, so I do not know how long the ruse will hold. Waking and seeing strangers could be a little unnerving for anyone. But I guess I can't minimize everything."

"And who, sir, are you in my bedchambers?" the President asked in a sleepy, but surprised tone. He was still feeling the effects of the sedative, so that lessened his alarm. Zeke and Miles were in their modern-day clothes, and they were much more alarmed than he was. So much for that ruse.

"Sir, Vice President Adams has asked us to tend to you, sir. You may not remember a fall you had from your horse, sir, and he was concerned," Miles said.

"John's a fine man. I must admit I do not remember falling at all. I feel drowsy though, perhaps that is a result."

"Sir, I am Dr. Leonard, and this is Dr. McDonald. We are here to help orientate you, sir, as you get your wits about you. I hope you will forgive any discomfort we have caused."

"No, it's perfectly all right, but I need to use the necessary, so if you could give me a hand up."

"I have this here, sir, for you to use, as we do not want you walking outside as of yet." Zeke said as he reached under the bed. The bed pan was right where he had told Peters to place it.

"If you'll excuse me gentlemen, I must get my wits about me," the President said.

"Oh yes, sir, we will be right outside your door."

As they left, the President rose and sat on the side of the bed.

He pulled up his nightshirt and relieved himself. He looked at the night shirt and thought he had never had such fine material before. He looked around his room. It looked familiar, but something was off. He got up, unsteady on his legs. Over in the corner was his desk. He walked over to it and opened the top. There was nothing inside. None of his writing materials, no paper. He then quickly surveyed the rest of the room. The vase Martha had placed in the room several years ago was not there in its place.

Wasn't he supposed to be in Philadelphia? Maybe the bang on the head had him out for a while, and these small issues had been changed by his staff.

"Gentlemen, please enter. I am confused, still," Washington yelled out. "I beg of you, sirs, I don't know if the fall has caused me harm, but I do not recognize all of this room. It has caused me much consternation," the President said as he continued to survey his surroundings.

"Mr. President, please take a seat," Zeke said. "I have to explain something to you."

Washington walked over to a chair next to the bed and sat down. He was looking at Zeke rather suspiciously. Miles and Zeke dragged two chairs from the side of the room and sat opposite the President, who had a stern and worried look on his face.

"And in what of these garments thou art both dressed upon? They are most peculiar," the President observed.

"Mr. Washington, I have to tell you a fantastic story. At first you will not believe it. It will seem too incredible. But I assure you, sir, everything I am about to tell you is the absolute truth, so help me God. We are both scientists, with well beyond the understanding of your old, departed friend Ben Franklin. We have learned things about the human body that were beyond the understanding that you had in your time."

"In my time sir, by what do you mean sir, in my time?" Washington asked.

"I'm not sure if anyone of your time thought about or talked about time travel in a fantastic way—about the ability to travel from one time to another, to go into the past or into the future. Did people tell stories like that?"

The President was getting more and more uneasy. Miles was thinking they might have to sedate him again, and maybe even do so several times. This orienting the President to what was happening was even hard for Miles to hear, never mind how it would sound to a man from the eighteenth century.

"We would convene and review the history of battles and talk of how this or that could have been altered or done better. We studied the teachers of the past. But going back to that time is impossible. I do not believe in witchcraft, sir, but what you are talking about sounds like something that people of that persuasion would believe. Let me see my servants and Martha now. This has gone on long enough." With that Washington rose.

"We have travelled you to another time, Mr. President. I know it is hard to believe, but it is science, not witchcraft that has allowed this time travel to occur," Zeke said in the calmest voice he could muster.

With that the President stood, walked across the room and reached for the door to the rest of Zeke's house. He swung open the door and stood there and stared in shock.

He first noticed an electric light on the ceiling of the living room. He had never seen such a bright light without a flame. He surveyed the rest of the room. Everywhere were fabrics and furniture of styles that were unfamiliar to him. Colors, shapes, lights are all different. He turned and looked back at Zeke.

"Sir, I beseech thee what have you done to the President of the United States? I must lead my nation. What are they to do if I am wherever I am? This is impossible. Have I been kidnapped? I demand to know what is going on!" The President was agitated, at the point of anger.

"Please, sir, let me explain more fully.

"You have not been kidnapped. To fully explain this to you I would like you to get dressed. Do not worry about the country. It is in good hands, and you have done the best job. I will explain that, too. Please get dressed. We have clothing over in the closet for you. I am going to take you to my laboratory and explain how all this has happened. I promise you; you will have a complete understanding when I have finished. Please, sir, give me a chance to make this clear to you."

"As I look around, sir, I do not seem to have a choice. I would run out of this room, sir, but to where?"

Washington stared for a minute, a full minute, and then turned and walked over to the closet. Zeke noticed the erect bearing he had in his posture. Obviously, he was a military man. As Washington opened the closet, he looked at the styles of clothes he had never seen. He carefully surveyed the clothes. He noticed a metal thing in his pants where buttons should be. A tie had a tag on it that said, "Rayon," a new and unfamiliar word. He slowly put on the clothes.

After he got dressed, he looked like an executive from Wall Street, sans tie, as he did not know what to do with that item. Zeke again assured him this matter would all be cleared up in the next half hour if he could just bear with him. For some reason Washington trusted the young man. He reminded him of Lafayette. But he spoke in unfamiliar phrases.

He could easily understand the English, but it was not what he was used to hearing.

Then he became calm, in what was an undeniably stressful situation. Many times in history it was noted how calm Washington remained in the most trying military trials he led. To Washington, something this young man was saying was, in fact, reassuring, during the most bizarre experience he had ever had. So, he was calm. But also troubled. He had been in many battles, and these experiences had conditioned him to keep his bearings when everyone else was losing theirs.

As they walked through Zeke's house, Washington noted all the strange things inside this place. He could only identify half the things he saw. And the simple things, like what appeared to be a stove, were beyond recognition. How did it work? There was no place to load the wood. That lamp—how did it glow like that? If all this were real, and Washington was not one to think he was in a dream, then indeed something very strange had happened to him.

They exited the house. Washington was looking for a horse or a carriage. Instead, this metal beast on wheels was waiting for him. Miles swung the door open for him. As he climbed into the front seat, he rubbed his gums. His false teeth were nowhere to be found. His gums were not as sore as they usually were, but they were starting to get to him. Zeke started up the van. He watched Zeke put on his seat belt, and so he looked for one, found his, and snapped it in place.

Washington could feel the engine operate, the vibration. The sound and vibration were new to him. He watched as Zeke put the van in reverse and backed out of the driveway. This amazing vehicle was moving without a horse to pull it. Incredible.

"You have time-travelled me into the future, haven't you, young man?" Washington asked as he surveyed the house and yards of the neighborhood.

"What are those poles and wires above our heads? Washington thought. Zeke noticed, and said, "Those are electrical power lines. They bring power around the country. With electricity harnessed, we can power lights in our homes and motors to run all sorts of equipment in our homes and businesses.  Like running a pump for a well.  Electricity is probably one of the most important power sources for the average man." Zeke then put the car in drive and took off. Washington had never traveled at a speed beyond twenty or thirty miles an hour. The trees and houses were whizzing past him at a speed he could hardly imagine.

"Exactly how fast are we traveling, young man?" the President asked.

"We are traveling at fifty miles per hour, sir. Vehicles like this can go over a hundred miles per hour."

"A hundred miles per hour!" The former president sat back and shook his head. What was he involved in here? He was feeling out of control, which made him uneasy. What was all this about, why had this happened? He watched as trees and houses whizzed by at speeds he could never have imagined.

He saw a woman and children standing by the road. A light turned red, cars from both directions stopped, and the group crossed the street.

Then the light turned green, and the cars all started up. The simple coordination of this event fascinated him. How did the object glow in different colors? As they moved along, he noted these electrical wires everywhere above his head. He noticed the smooth roads and wondered what they were made of. And they seemed to lead everywhere.

Suddenly an eighteen-wheeler passed Zeke's car. This massive piece of metal had wheels as large as Zeke's van. Washington was startled, almost disoriented by all this speed and movement. He was beginning to feel ill from all the chaos and confusion.

Zeke slowed the car down and turned into the industrial park where his lab was located. Zeke pulled into the front of his lab. He brought the car to a stop. Miles jumped out of the back seat and opened the President's door. Washington, with his military bearing swung out of the car and stood erect looking around.

Sensing Washington's increased agitation, Miles bowed and said simply, "Know that you are safe. We are here to help you figure out this situation."

They led the President to the laboratory's entrance, unlocking the big green steel door. The President strode in, his formal military bearing intact.

"Is this where you create the time travel you have spoken of?" the President asked, as he looked around at the pieces of equipment that were a marvel to him.

"In a way, sir. There is more to explain. You are now living in the twenty-first century," Miles said.

"The twenty-first century. This is incredible," the President said with some panic in his voice.

Zeke continued, "You are considered the father of our country. So, while you don't know us, we know much about you. You have had an extraordinarily successful Presidency. It's been over for over two hundred years. Many of your decisions on how to comport oneself in the Presidency are followed to this day.

"Our Constitution is still in place now with thirty-three amendments. We are the strongest and most wealthy country in the world. We are an empire stronger than England was in your day but without colonies. You got here by science.

"In the twenty-first century we have discovered the secrets of the human body. It is what we call the human genome. You do not know of human cells in your time, but medical science has learned that our bodies are made up of billions of cells, and the DNA in those cells tell them how to work.

"Do you have any questions at this point?" Zeke felt like a teacher who was going too fast, and whose student was going to fail the test.

Washington had walked over to the birthing chamber, stood by it, and listened to Zeke carefully. To think he has been transported over two hundred years into the future was hard—no impossible—to grasp. But look around him. Nothing was from his time. The beasts he rode in were all over the roads, as they drove to get to this place. He could not question any longer where he was, but how had this young man gotten him here and why?

"Why have you done this to me, Doctor? If I am so revered as you say, how could you do this to me? Am I still in another time existing, and have I gone missing?"

"Here goes," Zeke thought to himself. "The time you remember is no longer. It is past history. This is not time travel.

Sir, your original being is no longer. We have gotten your DNA, your cells of which I spoke, that ingredient that makes us who we are, and through my equipment in the lab, we brought your DNA to life.

I did not raise you from the grave, so do not think of it that way. I took the key to life that you had left behind on the sheet you died on in 1799, and I recreated you as you were in 1795. Subsequently, you do not remember anything beyond that date.

"This," Zeke said, pointing to the birthing chamber, "is where your DNA was taken and used to recreate you."

Washington had been stunned and confused by the time travel that this man Zeke had spoken of, but now this discussion of cells and DNA was truly beyond his comprehension. He could not make the leaps that Zeke was asking because too many pieces of science did not exist back in his world.

For Washington, the matter boiled down to the question: was he alive, or was he dead? Those are the only two conditions he knew about, life and death. And now, it seemed, he was both. He needed some time. Everything seemed real yet unreal. He turned and sat in Martha's chair.

It was obvious nothing else needed to be said at this point. In the matter of forty-five minutes, he had been catapulted into a new reality. For a full thirty minutes, no one spoke. Washington tried to capture the words he had heard and give them some understanding.

He was trying to understand how he could have died in 1799 and be alive again now. And that this experience really is happening to him. But how does one look at the future in two hundred years and get it?

People of a scientific age understand the world around them can change indescribably in a few short years, but it is much harder for someone from a time where little changed for generations. Where Washington had come from, people used flint locks for rifles, thought slavery was the normal course of events, rode horses to wherever they had to go, and died of simple infections because of the lack of antibiotics or even the knowledge of what an infection was.

Things had been the same for hundreds of years. Advancements within a lifetime were minimal. Scientific and medical knowledge was minimal. Washington's own death was hastened by doctors who bled him off half his body's blood, thinking it would help him recover from what was most likely an acute bacterial infection. How could he grasp DNA? Who in this current day would believe this clone of Washington if they reached out and touched him?

Zeke understood all this would be difficult, perhaps impossible to believe.

But as it unfolded, he began to realize what he was asking of Washington or anyone brought forward. He began to worry that his plan was all going to fall apart. Maybe he had made a mistake trying to bring an eighteenth-century man two hundred years into the future.

Maybe psychologically Washington would not be able to comprehend what was happening around him. Zeke was afraid the President could have a nervous breakdown—that the experience would be too overwhelming. Miles grabbed Zeke and stepped to the side of the room.

"This may be all too much, Zeke" Miles said. "I can hardly believe what's going on here, and I am a scientist of today, of this century. Maybe we made a big mistake. We knew your work had to be destroyed. This is why. It is unnatural. If it's unnatural for us to watch this, how do you think it is for the subject? Look at you. How did you feel knowing you had died? Your life is over, but now this other copy of you is alive and well. What is that knowledge doing to your brain?"

Zeke looked worried, knowing what Miles was talking about. He said, "I think I handled the shock at first because I completely understood what had happened as I read my notes. Not knowing about electricity, cars, or anything from our world is just piling on a stressed-out brain, I agree. Remember that while Washington was self-educated, he displayed an exceptional intellect during his time. The system of government he was a part of creating piece by piece has survived over two hundred years. Maybe we are underestimating him. I hope so, but I agree this is much harder than I expected."

Zeke and Miles stepped back by the birthing chamber and waited. Finally, Washington stood up and walked over to the birthing chamber.

"So, I am to believe this is my new mother? This metal and glass womb. If true, I do believe this is an abomination to God's plan and God's will," Washington said in a quiet, even tone. "How can you well-educated men commit such a horror? Never mind the 'science,' as you call this. Do you not have any ethical standards? If what you say is true, where is my soul? Tell me where my soul is?"

Miles stood and walked up to Washington. He stood only a few feet apart. He looked up at this great man. Washington's blue-grey eyes were steady, looking into Miles's eyes. Washington waited patiently. He was so elegant in his bearing, almost regal.

"I believe that God creates all things. I believe that nothing happens in this world, this universe that is not part of his plan. I do not know why Zeke was given this skill, this knowledge to do what he has done. But I do think this is God's plan.

"You and I are his tools. Our country, the country you helped create is in trouble. It needs a savior or all the work you did, that James Madison did, or John Adams, or Thomas Jefferson did will be lost. So, through some strange act that we can't fully understand, you are here. This is God's plan. He has placed you here with your soul. Now to do His bidding."

Washington continued to stare into Miles's eyes long after Miles had finished his speech. Neither moved nor shifted their gaze for what seemed like an eternity. Finally, Washington spoke.

"A Higher Power is something that I feel has guided me my entire life. Having acknowledged that this is real is still difficult for me. I have been thinking about Martha and all my friends and realize if what you say is true, they are gone. They were all alive, the last I knew, but now gone, all gone. And so now I am lamenting their loss. My whole life, I believed that God's hands would deliver us to freedom and that He was our savior."

He hesitated again and paused for ten minutes, then said "How can I question that now? While this upends my understanding of life and has brought despair to my being and changed my understanding of death and the afterlife, I must begin to assume that God has reinserted me here, with my soul, for a reason. I pray to God.”

And with that Washington lowered his head and turned away. He walked to a corner of the room and quietly grieved all he had lost.

Zeke now stood and said, “I do not know why I was driven to do what I have done. I was told by my wife it was wrong. Society said it was wrong. I am a good God-fearing man. But I persisted. But now it all makes some kind of strange sense.

“I could bring my wife back who has died. I miss and love her so much. But I know in my heart she would feel like you that it would be a mistake to do this for selfish reasons. So, I won’t. I cannot do it. But you sir, you have a purpose. One that could save a nation from itself. I am sorry for disturbing your eternal sleep, I really am.”

“I need more time, time to share my thoughts with my God. Please, let us return to your home, so I may have some time.”

With that, Washington left for the door. All three men got into the van and headed from Zeke’s home. Not a word was spoken on the way to Zeke’s home.

When they arrived at the house, Washington went directly to his room without speaking. Miles made some food and delivered it to his room, but other than handing him a tray no words were spoken. Zeke went to the family room and then called Peters.

“I’d like you to arrange to have the laboratory dismantled, and all equipment destroyed. There is a metal salvaging company in Windham. Arrange to have the equipment taken there and crushed into scrap. I would like you to call the scrap yard and have them expect your arrival. I want them to immediately destroy this equipment in your presence. I have the book of notes you gave me from the plane. I will destroy them myself.

"Are you aware of any copies?"

"To the best of knowledge, Zeke, those notes were taken from your lab and turned into the confidential booklet you have. No copies were made by me and that booklet was always in Jim's control until Jim gave it to you on the plane to read and then flown back to Boston."

"Good," Zeke said. "Please start as quickly as you can. Call me when it is done. I will then be in touch for a meeting in several days or a week or so. Thanks, Peters for your help."

Zeke hung up the phone. Never in his life was he so relieved as at that moment.

CHAPTER 12

## Now I Present to You …

Miles and Zeke kept making meals as they waited. Washington found the attached master bedroom bath and made full use of it, especially enjoying the hot water that was there with a turn of the faucet. On the third day of Washington's hiatus, Zeke knocked on the door.

"I am going to set something up for you. It is a film, a recording of events. It is a technology that we have. It is a brief overview of our American history and an overview of world- wide events. This second film is an overview of inventions during the nineteenth and twentieth centuries. If I may, I will set this up and play these for you. Also note the type of English spoken today."

Zeke showed Washington how the DVD worked and started the first film. It started with a picture of Washington. The President sat down and began watching the film as Zeke left the room.

The films were over four hours each. It was a little past noon the next day when Washington opened the door to his bedroom and joined Zeke and Miles in the living room.

"Do you have any lunch?" the President asked.

"All made. Spaghetti and meatballs. It's a recipe my wife made for me." Zeke said as he spooned out a heaping for his two guests. They all then sat down at the kitchen table and began eating without speaking. Finally, Washington broke the silence.

"Am I the only person who has been reconstructed with this DNA?"

"No. I am also a subject. We two are the only people who have been reconstructed and brought back in this way. I was dying from an accident in my lab. I was able to take my DNA and place it in the birthing chamber before I died, and here I am. Again, something which I had not imagined happening to me did happen. Why? I assume to bring you back. Otherwise, I don't know why I am here," Zeke said.

Washington let Zeke's words sink in and fade, then changed the subject.

"I was pleased to see that slavery has been stopped in this country. I had hoped that legislation would have ended it gradually and as the slaves were freed be returned to Africa. The deep south or where I lived, the Tidewater area would not join the Union if we even considered phasing out slavery. So as wrong as it was, I did nothing to end it. Not even on my own plantation. I've reflected on this now and feel it was the biggest failing of my life. Now I see over six-hundred thousand deaths occurred in a terrible civil war to end it.  How horribly I failed!

"I started to see slavery as wrong, as I grew older, but I saw no path forward on how to end it. I intended to free my slaves after Martha's death, but I see from history that only a few were freed.

"Lafayette used to counsel me that slavery was not the normal nature of man, as many of us thought at the time. I am surprised the country survived the Civil War. And this man, President Lincoln, seemed to change over time and realized it had to end. Once and for all. He had such a tragic death but the bravery to do what was right. Not doing anything to end it is a stain on my soul. Then more carnage in the next century. The first and second world wars. I always preached to John Adams, and he agreed with me, no foreign entanglements with these European countries. Their kings were at war forever. I understand we are now a world power, is that true?"

"Yes, we are arguably the strongest country in the world," Zeke said, "With technology that leaves many countries behind in our dust. But we have problems now. Big problems. In an effort to make a more fair and equitable society, we destroyed the middle class and made almost everyone poor. The middle class was formed mostly after World War II. Most Americans were of good health and income. Not rich, but not poor. They were able to buy things they needed and things for pleasure. This spending created the largest economy in the world, over sixteen trillion dollars a year.

"Our recent government wanted more of a European socialist structure, but what has happened is that we have inflation out of control, low production from our factories, and no jobs for the common man. We need someone to lead us back up on the path we should have never left. But before we get into the details of all of that I think we need to spend some time orienting you to this century.

"Also, I would like to give you an alias for now and try to disguise you. Your face is pretty well known, you know."

"I've seen a lot on your TV set, as you called it. I saw the weapons of war that the world has developed. It was frightening, the power. I am still trying to orient myself. I am still trying to convince myself I'm even supposed to be here and that I am not in a dreamlike state. After lunch I would like to take a walk. I often rode my land to survey the crops and visit with my workers. I feel I need some exercise."

"Do you want me to accompany you, sir? To explain what you might be seeing?" Miles offered.

"No, I need to be left to my own thoughts, Miles. I will be fine." And with that Washington finished his lunch, got up, and left the house. He took a left down Reed Street towards Main Street.

Reed Street had its beautiful maple trees lining each side of the road, all in brilliant fall colors. Washington breathed in the fall air. It was icier than Mount Vernon, but it reminded him of Valley Forge in Pennsylvania and a winter when he wondered if they would all survive.

But that was long ago now, much longer ago than he could fathom. So, he simply enjoyed the fall weather.

As he reached Main Street, there was a middle school on his left. Children were out on recess and he watched them for a while. He was aware that he may have been somewhat of an odd site. While he wore contemporary clothes, his brown hair was drawn into a ponytail in the back.

He still had no teeth, and his cheeks were sunken a bit. He wandered down Main Street and came to a gas station. He wondered what a gas station was. He walked up to the pumps where an elderly lady was pumping gas into her car.

"How do you do, madam? I am sorry to bother you, but can you tell me what you are doing? What is the hose connected to?" Washington stood tall asking his question in the most courteous but formal manner.

"What's wrong with you? What do you mean what am I doing? I'm just pumping gas into my car," she stated, as if he had been accusing her of stealing the gas.

"I'm sorry, madam, I didn't mean to offend you, but I have never seen this before. Does this gas make this metal beast run? I suppose it does. It has a rancid smell, don't you think?" Washington wrinkled up his nose as he spoke.

"I guess. I'm used to it, fella. Do I know you? I seem to have seen you before. I love the smell of gas, actually. I used to go around just smelling the fumes from gas tanks until my mother told me it would kill my brain cells each time you do that. But I didn't care, I kept sniffing anyway."

"Well, thank you, madam. I am learning a lot about cells lately. I hope your brain cells are all right and properly aligned," George said, as he headed into the store. The convenience store was all new to George. Rows of little packages of food and snacks filled the shelves. Washington wandered over to the coolers and opened the door. The coldness that came out surprised him. He turned to the clerk and asked, "Where do you keep the ice to keep your items so cold?"

The clerk, who was a black man, got a surprised expression on his face and said, "Oh no, sir. We use electricity to run compressors that keep the area cool."

"Compressors, you say. Can I see them?"

"Oh, they are on the back of the building outside. Please don't touch them," the clerk said, wondering who this tall guy was and what his problem was.

With that Washington went outside and around to the back of the building to look at the compressors.

He was impressed with the operation of these mechanical devices. The fans were whirling and humming away. He could see the blades turning and blowing out warm air. Shaking his head, he decided to move on.

After his tour of the convenience store, inside and out, he headed up the street to the downtown area. He passed a couple of teenage girls who were dressed, from their view, like Lady Gaga. George could not help but notice that they were scantily dressed, and as they walked by, he wondered if they were ladies of the evening, selling their wares. But they looked so young, it was confusing.

At this point Zeke caught up with Washington and eased up next to him in the van. He parked the car, got out and started to walk with him.

"What do you think of the twenty-first century, sir?"

"I'm not sure yet, Zeke. I was dealing with a man—I assume he was a freed man—who told me about compressors being used to keep things cold. That is quite an invention. But the ladies I have seen or met make me curious. They are wearing so little clothing. Is this normal?"

"Yes, sir, it is. The country is much more liberal today in its social mores than in your society. It is much less formal. And that is not a freed man. As you saw in the film, we had a Civil War that freed all African Americans over 170 years ago."

"Oh, that is correct. I need to remember that. It is not difficult for me to accept this end of slavery, as we discussed it, that idea, during the Continental Convention.

"As a southerner, I worried that the former slaves would not know how to take care of themselves if they were all made free at once. And many areas of our country could not accept this. Mainly because slavery was the labor actually created there's societies structure. The plantation owners, white farmers and slaves. They, we, considered ourselves the educated patricians of our society. And we did not want to change that, the country, we felt, needed that structure.

"The Puritans up in New England were disgusted by this thinking. And there was an argument by some that slavery was the proper order of man. It had been part of the Greek and Roman societies and the rest of the world for thousands of years. I am so relieved to learn about what came to pass, the end of slavery. I am glad it is over, and I hope in all other nations it has ended, too," Washington said wistfully.

"It was difficult for the ex-slaves and their next generations." Zeke added. "While they were no longer slaves, laws were enacted in many states to keep them down, not allow them to become part of society. The next hundred years were almost as bad as being slaves. Almost, but not quite." Zeke said, trying to explain two hundred years of difficult, painful history as they walked together.

"Is it better for them today? Washington asked almost anxiously.

"Yes and no. It is still not where it needs to be. Much better. Sometimes institutional racism continues, and it taints people's attitudes, creates misconceptions. But most Americans embrace equality for all, embracing Jefferson's words in the Declaration of Independence. That *all* men are created equal. And all the federal and state laws now promote this policy. Even though it is much better today, I don't want you to think the job is done. It's not," Zeke said. To himself he thought, "How can I get this right? I need to get this all right. The education of an eighteenth-century man—it was a big, big challenge, never before attempted.

Was it going to be impossible, too complicated?" He was starting to fear that it might be.

As they continued their walk through the streets of downtown, Washington was taking it all in—trucks and cars passing by, people and their clothing, and bits of overheard conversations, the ways people addressed and talked to each other. Everywhere he observed a much more casual and informal way of acting than he was used to. Public life and interactions seemed more open and relaxed, less constricted, than in his time, which felt disquieting. As they approached Zeke's favorite pub, Zeke asked his guest if he'd like a drink. Washington said yes, gratefully, that he would enjoy that. They walked in together and found a seat in the corner. At least pubs did not appear tremendously changed.

The barmaid, Wendy, came right over, happy to see Zeke. After greeting them, she asked for their drink order.

"What type of stout do you have, my lady?" Washington asked.

"Stout, hmm, I guess that would be Guinness. Well, we carry thirty-two types of beer. Here is a list. We also have ten types of bourbon, whiskey, gin—pretty much anything you would like."

After reviewing the list, he saw something he knew. "I will have a Sam Adams. He was a courageous man. I'm glad to see his namesake with a good family business," George said, as he handed Wendy back the menu of beers. "And I'd like some food. Do you have some mutton or pigeon for meat? And do you have some fruit?"

"No, sir, no mutton, no pigeon. I can make you a juicy hamburger. And I have some fresh pineapple. Would that work for you?" the waitress asked.

"Yes, I will try it with my Sam Adams," Washington said.

"And I'll have a per . . ." Zeke started to say.

"I know, Dr. Leonard, a perfect Manhattan with a cherry. Coming right up, gentlemen."

"I see this is your usual spot, Zeke. It is a pleasant little pub. With a nice barmaid. She is beautiful. And all the choices on the menu. This must be a special place."

"This is something you are going to have to understand. American people, in general, have choices of food and drink that even kings of old could never have dreamed of. Fresh fruit in the winter. Specialty foods brought in from other countries. Hundreds of varieties of beer competing against each other for business.

"The vast prosperity of this country has, on the whole, created a place on earth that you could have only dreamed of in your time. We have our very wealthy, and in the past a strong and large middle class, and, of course, the poor. Not poor like your day but considered poor. That is the way it has been for a long time, until recently. In an honest effort to make the middle class even bigger and better taken care of, our government started to think aspects of socialism would create a fairer country. But that has failed for a host of reasons.

" Now the middle class is decimated. We are becoming a county of rich and poor, with none in the middle. We need to get people in office who can put in laws and policies that get us back to a strong middle class. That is why you are here." Zeke said.

"I have been thinking about what the purpose is of all of this. Am I just an unwilling subject of an experiment that is . . . well, horrible? I should be at rest and done. But I am not. I am the one who never dwells on what should have been. So, I will not mention that I should not be here again. But why am I here, Zeke? Why?"

"A small group of us and a former president felt we could best effect change if we had an unquestionable dynamic leader. That this person could lead a new party away from the policies that have gotten us in a bad place and set us on a course of a healthy country. Someone like you."

"Zeke, first of all, I abhor the idea of leading a political party. I warned everyone against such things. I saw them as self-serving groups, putting man's wants and desires before the country. Second of all, yes, I was the leader everyone came to for help. But I was not a dynamic speaker. I saw the history tapes you provided me and saw those cousins Teddy and Franklin Roosevelt speak and marveled at their skill. And Ronald Reagan spoke as well as Shakespeare. I was never that person.

Wendy delivered their drink and food and left without a word, seeing the two in deep conversation. But trying to listen for her boss even though she did not understand all that was spoken.

"I spoke through my actions and writings so that my carefully chosen words would, I hoped, set this new nation on the right path. And look at me. I scare myself when I realize what I am. How would everyday people react to me? Frightened, I suspect," Washington said, as he drank his Sam Adams beer.

"You'd be surprised what people adapt to in this technological age that we live in. But that's not the point. We would change your appearance. First, we would get you some teeth—see a dentist for false teeth. This option will be quicker and with less discomfort than dental implants. Second, bring your hairline forward a bit and style your hair in the look of today. You would be unrecognizable at that point. We have the new Independent Party set up in all fifty states. We have current senators and representatives ready to leave the Democratic and Republican parties and join us. That is the current parties by the way. No more Whigs. We just need a leader to guide us as we bring this country back to its roots." Zeke thought for a second and added, "Back to its roots with the thirty-two amendments added to the Constitution and with the social change that has occurred in the country over our history."

"If I am going to stay, I could use some teeth," George agreed, zeroing in on that part of what Zeke had said. "I hope they are better than what I had. But so much is different from my time. I cannot walk down the street and not be bewildered by this new world. Just yesterday I stood for 15 minutes in the shower, thrilled by the endless hot water discharging. I went into your library and saw a writing instrument I had never seen before. I pushed the button on the top and a small metal point came out, and I wrote with it. Ink that did not smudge. If a writing instrument is startling to me, what would I do in a debate of different ideas, which I rarely had to deal with while I was President?"

Zeke realized he was probably right to a certain point. It might take a long time to bring George up to speed and also to understand all the political nuances of this modern world. Again, he thought this effort could be all a pipe dream.

"George, you, me and Miles are going on a road trip. Our trip will have as its goal the education of the new George Washington. Miles is astute in understanding the current political climate and drawing a good picture of American society today. By the time we get done, let us see how you are feeling and adjusting. Fair enough?" Zeke asked, staring at the President.

They finished their drinks and George's first hamburger, which he pronounced the best sandwich he had ever had. After walking back to the van, they drove to the house, where George excused himself to watch the history videotapes again. There was much to learn.

That evening Zeke called Miles. Zeke asked him to please take a leave of absence for at least three weeks, the planned duration of the road trip.

Miles told him he had informed the department head he was taking a year's sabbatical. They didn't like the short notice, but they relented. He asked Miles to bring all the literature and other materials he thought might help in the education of our late great president. Zeke summarized their urgent mission: to bring the President into the 21st century.

And later that day, a cell phone arrived and given to the president. They explained it to him, and he simply stuffed it into his jacket pocket.

Two days later the three men stared at a rented American Coach RV. It had two bedrooms and a convertible couch. Miles and Zeke would fight over the couch while George had the master bedroom with a bath.

Zeke felt traveling this way would allow them more flexibility to go where they wanted to go and settle wherever they were each evening. When a man from the local rental company dropped off the RV, he showed them how to operate the coach's amenities. It had a pop-out feature which, when parked, almost doubled the width of the living room. It had flat screen TVs in every room, a full kitchen, and even a wine refrigerator.

This RV would work out perfectly. George was impressed.

Before they left, Zeke and George drove into Boston for the important appointment with a prosthodontist, who said he could make a set of dentures for George in one day and fit the patient painlessly.

Zeke took Route 93 into the city, encouraging George to ask any questions he might have along the way. Zeke didn't want to assume George "understood" what an eighteen-wheeler was, for example. And George had many questions— "What is that huge truck carrying? Where is it coming from and where is it going? Who owns it? Who is driving it?" Zeke told about the nation's supply chain that was supported by trucking systems. He tried to give a brief picture of the fleet of drivers, the variety of goods being shipped, the existence of refrigerated trucks, and all such points, while not bogging down in too much detail. The men found no end of topics to discuss.

As they approached Boston, George could see the skyline in the distance.

"Look at the size of the buildings," George said, surprised. "Is this one of the largest cities in America now?"

"Oh no, not by a long shot," Zeke said. "There are only about 650,000 people in Boston proper. There might be about 800,000 in the metropolitan area counting surrounding towns like Cambridge, Watertown, and Dorchester. By comparison, New York City has over eight million inhabitants. Los Angeles on the West Coast has about four million people."

"Los Angeles is in California, right? I read about that," George said. "I have read that we have explored and settled the whole country that form forty-eight contiguous states. That is incredible and only a dream in my time. I used to talk to Thomas Jefferson about how we could spread west and occupy the whole continent, especially with European countries claiming ownership of large swaths of the continent. I read how Thomas purchased the area called the Louisiana Purchase from Napoleon. I knew of Napoleon as a commanding general but not as the leader of France. When Benjamin got back from France after we signed the treaty with the King, we had no idea that France was going to have its own revolution. And then the Mexican American War gained the country a vast swath of the southwest of our country. I read about our thoughts that it was our "Manifest Destiny" to control the entire continent. Our Lord above could only have directed us in this effort," George said, shaking his head.

As they drove into Charlestown, Washington spotted the *USS Constitution*. "Is that what I think it is? It has survived all these years."

"Yes, it has. They take it out every year or so and turn it around. It is a popular tourist attraction. And if you look over to your left, you can see the Bunker Hill Monument, to signify that place of that battle," Zeke said, pointing out the passenger window of the car.

"Yes, Breed's Hill. We lost a number of good men in that battle. I was especially fond of Dr. Warren, whom I had met several years earlier. A particularly good man. I rode into Cambridge about a month after this battle to start organizing the

American army. That was in 1775. It was a time for planning. To see if a rebellion was even possible."

"I think that is what we are doing now, George. Planning. To see if this idea is even possible," Miles said.

Zeke pulled up in front of the dentist's office and took George inside. The receptionist was about twenty, and she barely looked twice at George. In her view, he was just a long-haired old guy needing teeth, as so many people did. The dentist immersed himself in George's mouth, bringing all his knowledge, experience, and art to the job.

After six hours they emerged with a different looking Washington. Before his cheeks had been sunken in, but now he looked like a more handsome and healthy man, or at least like a happy man who was thrilled with his new teeth. He kept looking in the car mirror marveling at the natural look.

"I had suffered for years with that contraption I used for teeth. They fit quite badly and could be painful. These feel wonderful. I would say I feel like a new man, but I guess I am already one of those, right, Zeke?" Washington smiled, showing all his teeth.

Zeke was pleased George had a sense of humor left at all.

"Yes, all new. Now for a haircut. Here is a barbershop right here. Walk-ins welcome. Let's walk in and get rid of that long, historic hair."

They went into the shop, and a small man of about sixty years old greeted them. "I guessah you have wantah to leave your hippie days behindah, or you just wanteh a trim?" the small round man said, with an Italian accent.

"I would like a modern haircut, sir. Cut this shorter for me if you would." As George sat down the barber showed him a picture of hair that was spiked, Mohawk-style, pointed out like a mad scientist, and purple.

"I see your name is Peter. Peter, these haircuts are interesting, but I would rather not have a Mohawk style. Although I have seen it in person. Peter, please give me a haircut like Zeke here." George said, pointing to Zeke.

"You knowah, youah look so familiarah to me," Peter said. "Are youah famous entertainer or something? You just have suchah a familiar faceah. I feel like I have seenah youah hundreds of times before."

Zeke thought to himself, "Sure … like on the dollar bill?"

"I swearah, I know youah from somewhere. It will come to me. I'mah good at placing people. I have hadah Celtic players here and figured outah who they were, but of course they are 6 feet 10 inches tall, so you knowah something up as soon as they walk in. But I hadah Sean Connery here years agoah, and I said to him, 'Hey, I know youah,' and he laughed. He was a good tipperah, too."

Peter paused, stared hard, and then said earnestly, "You knowah, if you had a white wigah on, you'd look like George Washington. Here lookah at this dollar bill. See the wigah. Man, youah look just like him. You should becomeah like an actor, you couldah probably get some pretty good gigsah coming in, all dressed up and all."

"What do you know about Washington?" George asked.

"Didn't you go to schoolah? Everybody knows about Washington. Even people in foreign countries today they knowah

Washington. He was the fatherah of our country. A revered general who won the Revolutionary War. Our first president. There is a lot of places around townah that say, "Washington Slept Here," as a point of pride, and people just wantah to see the rooms where he stayed. Why would you askah? You must knowah about him."

"Oh yes, I know him well. I was simply curious how you thought about him. I'm doing some work, studying our history, and wondering about your views of him." George sat back and let the barber do his work, as he chatted away.

He got a shave, too, and when Peter was done, George still resembled the Washington of old, but only if you were looking for it. He was sixty-five years old and looked tired, worn down. But his new haircut and teeth made him into a modern man of the day. It was just the look what Zeke was hoping for. They paid Peter and thanked him for such a good cut.

"I gottah tell you. You need to get an agent and get into the entertainment business. You could pull off imitating Washington at all kinds of corporate gigsah."

"Gigs, you say gigs?"

"Yeah, you knowah, jobs. Hey guys, thanks. It is good meeting you, George. I cannot wait to get home tonight and tell my wife. Can I get a picture with you?"

"A picture. What type of picture?"

"From my phone here. We take a selfie," Peter said.

"Maybe next time, Peter," Zeke said. He took Washington's arm and led him from the shop.

As they got into the van, Zeke said, "I don't think we are ready for a million questions, if your picture went on the internet."

"Internet? What is the internet? Oh, is that something to do with computers?"

"Yes. If Peter took your picture and posted it on the internet, millions and millions of people could possibly see that picture," Zeke explained. "Then they would-be all-over Peter to tell him about meeting you. Next, newspaper people or regular citizens would start to track you down and bother you with questions and requests for appearances. We don't need that kind of attention right now, agreed?"

"You will have to tell me more about this internet," George said. "It seems like a very powerful way to communicate."

On the way back to New Hampshire, they listened to CNN and Fox. As the two most prominent political stations, they gave George a good sense of the two sides of one story. While Fox denigrated President Bartlett and his failed policies, CNN lauded the changes and supported the idea that the country was just going through a transition from a Republic to a more equitable Republic/Socialist state.

A mixture that would work out with everyone better off, except for the rich. George noticed the virulent attack on successful people.

Since George was one of the wealthiest Americans of his time, he took special note of this attitude, and it worried him. If the ruling class, and there is always a ruling class, was going to be torn down and apart, what will fill that space? He listened, and all his instincts told him while a theoretical dream, socialism just does not end up working that way. He started to see what he was dealing with and the direction he had to try and get the country to move in.

# CHAPTER 13

# And We're Off!

That evening they gathered in Zeke's kitchen for dinner. Wendy called and offered to make dinner, and Zeke agreed. They were having boneless breast of chicken in a white wine sauce. Over the chicken was spinach and mozzarella cheese.

"This meal is sumptuous, Wendy," Washington said. "Thank you for this evening. Zeke's meals leave a lot to be desired," Washington said with a smile.

"You know, I resemble that remark!" joked Zeke. "Yes, thanks, Wendy. You seemed to know your way around the kitchen pretty well."

"I'm sorry you can't remember, Zeke, but, yes, I do know the kitchen here a bit. I am glad you liked it, George. Would you like some more summer squash?" At the end of the evening Zeke walked Wendy out and thank her for her help. "We should be back a few weeks Wendy, see you then," Zeke said. Wendy gave him a hug good-bye.  The three men then retired for the evening.

Miles, Zeke, and George headed out in the camper the next day. George could not get over his new teeth. The soreness had left his gums, and he thought he looked like a million bucks. He used to smile in a somewhat of a closed-mouth manner to hide his ivory false teeth or his set made from other men's teeth. Now he could smile naturally. And he could speak more easily, too, and less softly.

Part of the reason he was known for speaking softly was because his ill-fitting artificial teeth made talking difficult. His new haircut pleased him, too. He felt better than he had in years. He had reconciled himself to what had happened.

He had an abiding faith in God. His faith in the Lord had served him well all his life. Because of that, he could only feel it was the hand of God that had placed him in this present situation. Holding on to that faith allowed him to accept his current predicament.

Zeke on the other hand, while being a man of faith, did not have the life experiences and the deepness of George's unblinking devotion. He was having a harder time dealing with this situation they were both in. The loss of Jane was still new to him, as the loss of Martha was new to George.

Zeke had checked with Peters about the state of the lab. Peters assured him that all the equipment had been crushed into small metal squares and scrapped. The laboratory was now empty except for Martha's chair. The evening that the three of them got back from Boston, Zeke spent the night burning his notes in the big stone fireplace in the living room. He explained to George what he was doing and why. While his experiment had brought both George and Zeke a second chance, it was never going to be used again, Zeke swore. George was impressed with Zeke's righteousness, and it convinced him even more that the mission they were on was God's work.

And Zeke in turn was impressed by George's devotion. A secular being himself, he thought about how men of George's generation were, in general, deeply religious. The Protestant religion had entrenched itself in the America that George and his co-founders had helped to create. At times men's belief got in the way of equality and kindness to all human beings, but those contradictions were caused more by the frailty of man's character than the religion.

As they headed out on their long road trip, they decided the first stop on their journey would be New York City. They headed over to Jersey City and pulled into Liberty Harbor RV Park. It was a beautiful autumn day, and they decided to visit the Statue of Liberty and take a ferry to Manhattan.

"So, this was a gift from France to the United States," Miles stated, like the student of history he was. "As you know, Brissot and Robespierre were the most important leaders of this movement. Bonaparte established himself as emperor of France around 1800. In any event, this statue became a gift, thanking America for showing the world that men could free themselves from monarchical rule."

"This is quite a gift," George said.

"It has been a symbol of the American Dream to millions of people. New immigrants from around the world would travel by ship from Europe and stand on the decks in excited jubilation or crying in happiness in seeing this symbol of freedom. This is what our founders of this country did for the world, George. It was and is to this day a profound statement for the freedom of all people."

Washington stared at the statue and listened to Miles's comments. He looked around and saw the area a mess. Obviously, there was no money to maintain the property. Protesters with signs were located near the parking lot. Guards carry guns were everywhere.

Suddenly they heard a gunshot. Then several more shots. The guards ran toward where the shot had come from. People were screaming, "Down with Bartlett." The three men went behind the statues stand and took cover.

About 20 mins passed, and all clear was given by the police and guards. Things were getting worse by the day.

Washington said nothing and showed no emotion. But he was thinking of the day he travelled to New York so many centuries ago to give his inaugural address.

What a difference.

And he was thinking back to the men that he knew as comrades in arms on those days that seemed so bleak. And then to those men who worked tirelessly in shaping the constitution. John Adams, James Madison, Thomas Jefferson, and old Ben Franklin, not in good health, but still alert and engaged. They all struggled hard to create a more perfect union, and perhaps to a degree they had succeeded.

But now what? Then he turned and looked at the skyline of New York. If Boston had been amazing, New York was almost beyond his imagination in its scope and scale. How could this all start be falling apart at the seams?

"Let's go to the city," Miles added. "The ferry is getting ready to leave."

"How does this boat go? What power does it use?" Washington asked.

"It uses a combustion engine powered by diesel fuel. Both were invented or discovered during the nineteenth century. During the nineteenth and twentieth centuries, a whole shift occurred in how we powered our industries, means of transportation, and homes. Probably electricity, the power behind the light that you noticed and liked, was and is the key power source of the world. Where there once was darkness, there is light. Wait until you see the city at night."

"Ben used to talk about electricity and its power whenever the subject came up. He said he could see a world where electricity could be harnessed and work for mankind. He was such a visionary. And a good statesman. He got France to back our revolutionary efforts and frankly that made all the difference. Yorktown. I will never forget Yorktown, and the French troops and warships. We should have sent a statue to them!"

As they boarded the ferry, Washington took note of how people dressed and carried themselves. Some were well dressed, but most looked like beggars. Unkempt hair, dirty clothing. He noted the ferry and the men working the lines. As the ferry pulled into the Hudson, the power of the boat mesmerized him. He thought of what it would take in his day to traverse the Hudson. The ferry ride was a perfect way to see Manhattan.

Overhead the Verrazano Bridge was an immense superstructure, large both to him and to Zeke and Miles. But it needed maintenance. Paint was peeling off or completely gone from the superstructure.

He gazed up the Hudson and saw a bridge spanning from Manhattan to New Jersey, his namesake.

When they docked, Miles hailed a cab and asked to be taken to Central Park. He thought they would start at the park and walk south back to Times Square.

As they strolled down Broadway through the 50s, Miles kept a running dialog with George. He pointed out items along the way as an explanation of how things were changed from his time. Miles would sprinkle in historical context where he could keep George moving up through the nineteenth and twentieth centuries. There were disturbing signs all around them. They passed dozens, if not hundreds of people begging. About every third store was shuttered with spray painted slogans, "Free American from this tyranny." Instead of the sidewalks being a parade of fashionable dress, the clothes of passersby were shabby and disheveled. Garbage and wastepaper were everywhere, in piles and swirling in the wind. The city's services had collapsed. A man stopped them, "Hey buddy, can you give me a hand? I am a barber, but no one has an extra dime to get a haircut."

Thinking of their hardworking, friendly Peter, Miles gave the man some cash. As they continued down Broadway, the sun began to set, and the lights of New York came on. They entered Times Square, ablaze with large screens flashing the news and advertising everything you could imagine.

Much of it shocked Washington's sensibilities. Men in underwear, and women as well. There seemed to be no shame. They walked past 42nd street, and all the theatres had "CLOSED" on their marquee.

"What is pizza?" George asked, staring at the blazing neon lights everywhere. "I see it mentioned often in the signs of the shops,"

"It is an Italian dish that is popular here," Miles answered with a smile. "Let's get a slice and you can try it."

They all got slices of plain pizza, and George slowly nibbled one edge. His new teeth were working fine, and soon his eyes lit up, as the flavors of this delicacy hit his taste buds. The pizza parlor owner thanked them profusely for the $10.00 worth of business. It doubled her sales for the night, she said.

"This is excellent," George exclaimed. "You are right, Zeke. The choices Americans have been many, many more than I could have ever imagined. I can say that the foods I have eaten these last few weeks have pleased me greatly. But there is a big dichotomy, I see. The vestiges of society's wealth are disappearing before our eyes. On the ferry I heard people speaking of not having a job, that there were no jobs to be had. Another said they worked for the state, and people did not even show up for work and they got paid.

Another I heard say they were living in their car, and only 6 months ago they had a beautiful house on Staten Island.

One moment I see wealth and what this country was, and then next I see desperation. This country is in transition."

"When I rented the RV the man almost kissed me," Zeke said. "He said his business may not be open when we return, and if that is the case, we should just call him, and he will come and pick up the RV. It is like watching a balloon slowly leaking air. I think what we need to do is go to a political rally. There is one tonight in Washington Square.

"As you've noticed, George, your name is around a lot of places. There is a group of people meeting who are making the claim that opportunities for the average person are melting away as the new direction of the Federal Government takes root. Let us go to that and hear what they have to say."

They agreed this might be a good place to start. So, they stopped at a small Italian restaurant and had dinner. Afterward they took an Uber down to Washington Square. While this day has been quite a hike for Zeke and Miles, the exercise seemed to invigorate Washington.

He felt he needed to move, to help him clear his mind and continue to try and grasp where he was and why. It was still a struggle.

All he knew was gone. All his family and friends were gone. Everything that was familiar to him was gone. While he intellectually grasped the changes around him, emotionally it was taking a toll.

The same was true of Zeke.

He kept thinking that he should not be here. That if his faith were correct, he would be with Jane now. Was he with Jane now? As George had asked, where were their souls? These thoughts kept Zeke awake at night. His only solace was that his scientific notes and the equipment were gone. And even though he would acknowledge that, if he had done it, someone else could, too, he hoped no one would want to. He prayed that would be true.

As the day advanced, they walked into the square where about a thousand people had gathered. The crowd was made up of all types of people. It was truly a melting pot of many cultures, ethnicities, and races. Out of the crowd stepped a well-dressed man, of average height with brown hair and a small mustache. He appeared to be about thirty years old or maybe a little older.

"My fellow Americans, I come to you tonight to express my concerns to you. As our government has chosen to find solutions to our society's problems with a broad-brush stroke of socialist ideas, we have seen our wealth diminish. In the effort to create more equality in our society the Federal Government has undertaken a broad redistribution of wealth. Instead of making us all better off, we have all become worse off."

The crowd yelled its approval with comments like, "We must go back, and capitalism is what makes us great."

"We all agree we need to stop any nationalization of any more businesses. We must elect people who will reverse President Bartlett's agenda. Our best option is at the ballot box. There we can make our voices heard and stop this movement. Let us all reach our own individual greatness. We do not want the government in every aspect of our lives. This was never what the founding fathers envisioned."

Zeke and Miles looked at George upon this comment but saw no reaction.

"There is a new party forming. It is called the Independent Party of America or the IPA. We have enrollment forms here tonight for you to sign. If you believe that our best hope is to get both the Republican and Democratic parties out of the way, so we gain back the America we all know, then become a member of the IPA and let's change things one vote at a time."

The crowd erupted into applause.

The enrollment form passed around quickly as people signed their names, gave and phone number, address and email address. It seemed like everyone in the crowd was onboard with this change. The three men decided to leave after about forty-five minutes of more speeches.

They got down to the pier and boarded a ferry back to Jersey City. As he sailed across the Hudson, George stared at the shining skyline.

"What I heard and saw here was another revolution. That's why I am here. To lead another revolution. I can see my purpose. Zeke, this all did not happen by accident or coincidence. There are no coincidences," George said with conviction, more than he had shown to date.

As they entered a restaurant for an evening drink near the campground, they stepped into an elevator to go to the second floor.

"And what is this box with doors, gentlemen?" Washington asked.

"It's called an elevator. It can take us up one hundred floors if needed. It made traversing large skyscrapers like you saw in New York possible. We are only going up to the second floor right now," Miles said.

"Are stairs still in use, young man?" Washington asked sincerely.

"Oh yes. But in many public buildings, where there are many floors, elevators are used. It makes getting to the upper floors in a building easier for us, and it opens up those higher floors to handicapped people, too," Zeke added.

"How thoughtful," the President remarked, impressed by the inclusion demonstrated by the device.

As the elevator door opened and they stepped into the restaurant, Washington saw the skyline of New York across the Hudson River. Even to New Yorkers it was a spectacular view. He stood there for several seconds just taking in the enormous sight. A maître d' took them to a table that had a view of the city. As they sat, Washington spoke.

"What I am observing is the shell of a robust country. People seem to live with riches beyond my life experiences. Some are dressed well and clean. I notice their teeth are all well cared for, too. In my day, teeth were not good or fell out altogether. But most are so downtrodden. Nice teeth, but sad."

Miles wanted to help Washington grasp the troubles among the positives they see around them.

"It's the philosophical changes that are being put forward which are the danger," he said.

"In your day, you would never consider the Federal Government owning and operating large companies. This is happening today. You would never think of taxing people so punitively in an attempt to redistribute the wealth. You would never make men of wealth the enemy. These policies, these ideas have taken the backbone of our economy, the middle class, and decimated it. In this restaurant are only the most fabulously wealthy of our society. Normally it will be filled with people of the middle class. They do not exist anymore.

"About 80 percent of our economy is generated by the middle-class buying things for their lives. If they stop buying things factories close, restaurants close, automobile factories close, the companies who make the glass of automobiles close. It is a domino effect. So those factory workers can no longer survive as part of the middle class.

"The IPA's thought is if we can bring back capitalism and smaller Federal government then our current problems will correct themselves. But someone, an unquestioned leader needs to help to convince the people of the right path to follow. And that is why you are here."

"My understanding of small Federal government is probably much smaller than even yours. Beyond providing for the defense of the country and for the public good it had little else to do in every everyman's life. Thomas Jefferson took a different view, and he and I discussed this subject many times. But I agree nationalizing businesses and punitive taxes—imposed to move money around to other segments of the population—makes no sense unless it is to help the poor. But even then, it should be done on the state level or through our churches," George said with conviction.

"I think what we need to do is to let you absorb what you see and what other people tell you. So, let's not spend too much time on what we think and what we hope you can do. Over time, I think you will gather information and see if there is a path you want to take," Zeke said. T

As they shared a bottle of wine, they all began to relax. The whirlwind of all that had happened in the last weeks started to calm down as they sat at the table.

After a couple of hours, they went back to their RV and climbed in. The President excused himself and retired to his bedroom for the evening. He had been given a phone by Zeke, and he said he was expecting to make some calls. Who's calling him? Zeke thought. Zeke and Miles sat at the kitchen table and talked.

"This is so hard," Miles commented. "I hope he can help us. Somehow, some way."

"Me too," Zeke said as he noticed a small tremor in one of his hands.

"It is a giant problem bringing him into today's world. While we can point out how elevators work, how do you convey social mores and conventions that have changed so much? Did you see him in Times Square? He was appalled. I mean genuinely appalled," Miles said anxiously.

"I think in some ways the intellectual discussion of political structure is easier than explaining the world we live in. My thought is that we ask Peters to set up a string of political gatherings or town hall meetings, where we will have him, and others present the party's planks. Let Washington hear from the common man as he did back in 1790. Let him draw his own conclusions."

"Ok, I'll get a hold of Peters and tell him what we want," Zeke said. "We will lay out a trip down the Eastern Seaboard first and then across the southern part of the country. Getting off the highways and travelling through cities and towns will be more educational. We'll take our time to absorb what is around us. I'll call Peters now."

Zeke called Peters and described what he wanted to do, some regional meetings to discuss policy. Peters said he would have to talk to Jim Robinson, as Jim was taking the lead on this whole effort of setting up the party. Getting people to join the IPA was surprisingly easy. People wanted change back to what they knew.

As they discussed not jamming the trip with meeting after meeting, they thought maybe less was more. Talk to Jim, Zeke said to Peters, and let me know what he thinks. Peters was pleased to be hearing from Zeke and Miles.

He was still in the dark on how this "leader" of the party was going to be found, but he had faith in the two of them.

The next morning, they left New York City and headed south on 95 to Washington, D.C. George said little. He rode next to Zeke in this rolling cabin contraption called an RV, reflecting on the last few days. As they passed Newark Airport, Washington saw a jet take off and land for the first time.

"What is those hulking silver . . . things?" he asked with alarm.

"They are airplanes. Jets to be exact. Man learned how to fly," Miles said from the couch in the living area. "We started to learn how to fly about a hundred years ago. Over that one hundred years, aviation has advanced to the point that—hold onto your hat, Mr. President—we have sent men to the moon and back."

"I saw that in one of the . . . what is it called, films, you asked me to watch. But I must say seeing these planes in person is impressive. By the way, have you noticed that I am beginning to speak more plainly? Much like the both of you. I realized that evolution has affected our language as much as everything else. I have been studying the language by watching TV. It is a good teacher."

"I guess I hadn't noticed your adjustment. It shows how natural it has become for you, sir." Zeke said

The RV streamed along and after about two hours approached Washington, D.C.

"We want to pace ourselves to Charleston, South Carolina, in a couple of days. There is time now to look around Washington, D.C., if you would like, Mr. President?" Miles asked.

"I think I would like to take a look around. I laid the cornerstone of the White House, but I never saw this city finished," Washington said.

Zeke parked the RV in a public area for RVs about two miles from the White House. He took his phone from his pocket and summoned a Lyft car. Washington watched Zeke's phone as the Lyft car's driver's face appeared on the screen, with a message he would be there in three minutes. He then watched as the car depicted on Zeke's screen took a corner and approached the parking lot where they were located.

And then there he was. It was another thing that could seem remarkable, even to people of the modern day.

"We'd like to take a driving tour around town. We'll let you know when we want to jump out," Zeke said.

As they drove down Pennsylvania Avenue, they approached the White House. They stopped at a safe distance, and Washington got out to walk up to the fence around the sprawling grounds. Without saying anything, he turned and got back in the car. They went on to the Capitol. Same routine. Out, look around, get back into the car. Zeke pointed out the Washington Monument and Jefferson's statue. They then stopped next to the national mall, near Lincoln's memorial.

Again, Washington got out and walked along the mall and the reflecting pool, to the Lincoln memorial. He walked up the steps, stood in front of the impressive statue of the seated man, and read the Gettysburg address chiseled in one of the walls. He then turned and looked down at the Mall and the monument dedicated to him.

He turned to Zeke and said, "I think I like Lincoln's better," with a little smile.

They then went back to the RV and headed out of town. Zeke realized that for George, the visit was like when a person tries to go back to his old office after he's retired. Much has changed, and it's just not the same. There is no sense in being there anymore, no place or purpose anymore. While this city was all new to Washington, he did not want to linger long in a town that no longer included him, even one named for him.

By Monday late afternoon they pulled into Charlestown. They found a RV park and settled in for the evening. The next day was the IPA rally. They had been told by Jim Robinson that this event would be the official launch for the party. Jim had asked if they had found the person, they needed to introduce the party to the world.

A bit startled by the rapid events, Zeke said he was ready. They were all anxious to see what was going to happen

After a day of walking around Charlestown, the President was feeling good. The exercise was good for his body—he had always thrived on physical activity to stay fit. Since he did not have a horse to ride, walking was perfect for him. And he was anxious to see the rally that evening. It was said that fourteen thousand people had bought tickets to attend it. All the major news stations were there covering the event.

The three of them sat in the RV, and Miles started the conversation.

"George, we have got to think of a name for you so we can introduce you to different people."

"Use my name, Miles."

"I'm not sure we can, sir. We can't really explain where you came from."

"I will not lie, sir. I understand we cannot break to them the entire picture, as you say. It would be too alarming. But I will not use another name. I will not be an imposter."

Zeke thought about this point and paced back and forth a bit. Finally, he said, "Okay, Mr. President. If we may, we can just say you are a descendant of Augustus Washington since you had no children. But no other information."

Zeke called Trump's office. Explained what was happening. He needed help. He needed a backstory for Augustus Washington's lineage for the press to validate George as a person. Trump told him not to worry. It would be in place by the end of the day.

By mid-afternoon Peters called and met them where they were parked. He was interested in meeting this new fellow. Zeke had talked so much about him and so glowingly.

"Peters, this is George Washington. Kind of a famous namesake, wouldn't you say?" Miles said.

Peters did not know what to say. George turned to meet him. The older man's countenance and bearing were so . . . so presidential, so naturally dignified. Peters' was almost embarrassed for gazing at this remarkable man. And George had not said a word yet.

"How do you do, George? Are you related to *the* George Washington?" Peters asked.

"Yes, to his brother, so to speak," the President said.

Peters stared at him, too long for comfort. "You do carry some strong features that you can see in his portraits. But I see you have beautiful teeth, a vast improvement over those of the old George," Peters said with a laugh.

"Yes, I was blessed with these teeth. And of you, sir, what is your background?"

"I was fortunate to work for a great president, sir, Donald J. Trump. He did a remarkable job."

"Yes, I did see him profiled in an interesting History Channel program. He was a departure from what we had been used to in this country. There seemed to be a lot of turmoil around his presidency."

"Well, you must have seen that yourself, right, sir?"

"Oh yes, but having encapsulated it that way was, I thought, insightful."

"It's interesting, Zeke. You indicated the person you had in mind for the IPA was George Washington, but you were not kidding. George is a spitting image."

"He is, and that's why I said what I said. When I met George and listened to his thoughts on the state of the country, I thought to myself no one will believe this. But hey, I think when you hear George's ideas, you will be impressed," Zeke said.

After some small talk, the group sat down and got into the politics of the IPA and the meeting tomorrow night.

It was there in that discussion that Peters was blown away by Washington.

It is such an intangible, but it was there. This man was unquestionably a leader, used to being a leader. He commanded respect with his every word. He was firm, quite formal, but direct. He was exactly the person the party needed. Peters was relieved. How did Zeke find this guy?

They expected a big crowd, and all the major networks would cover it, but not live. CNN and FOX had committed to carry it live, with FOX saying they would feature the main speaker live. So, they would get some fairly good coverage for a new political party.

The IPA was not being taken too seriously by the main media, so far. Most of the senators and congressmen who indicated they would join a new party, if the planks of the party were as Jim Robinson had laid them out, indicated they would watch the meeting on TV. If they were in, they would text Jim and he could use their name. They were waiting to see what happened.

The Senators and Congressmen and women were putting their political careers on this line this evening.

After Peter's left, George excused himself. He needed to gather his thoughts and write. He was not designated as the main speaker in the program. Just another speaker.

They would all see what happened.

CHAPTER 14

# A Star Is Born

Zeke, Miles, and George were going to the stadium about two hours before the event started. Before they left George had spent three hours in his room. He asked not to be disturbed. Zeke had no idea what he was up to.

When they did arrive at the stadium there were already thousands of people milling around outside the gates to the stadium. The organizers had begun screening everyone who was entering and starting to fill the seats. George went in with Miles and Zeke.

After security had checked them, they went to the stage to get a sense of where things were located. The sound technicians were working on the sound. A small microphone was on one of the technician's headsets, and he was talking normally into the mike.

The technician's voice boomed around the stadium, and George was fascinated by the amplification.

"I cannot believe my ears. I was thinking about why I have such a large space. Beyond ten or twenty rows, who was going to hear anything? I expected most people to read the speeches in the newspapers. And that may happen, but all in this stadium will hear every utterance."

"Yes, George. Let's let you have a try," Miles said.

He asked one of the technicians if a speaker could try a microphone, explaining, "He's not spoken with this type of equipment before."

George put the headset on and looked up into the slowly filling seats. He said, "Hello, my name is George Washington. I welcome you here this evening." He took off the headset and walked away.

Someone yelled back, "Yeah, and I am Abe Lincoln. Nice to meet you, George."

"This microphone will fit in your ear, George. Here try it." Miles said as he adjusted it in George's ear, "Now I am going to speak to you from across the room."

Miles walked across the stage. He whispered into the microphone.

"Testing, George, can you hear me?"

"That is remarkable," George marveled.

"If I need to tell you anything during the speech, I can whisper it to you. That is what this is for," Miles said.

George turned and went directly to the dressing room, before closing the door he turned and said, "I have to make a telephone call and have a long conversation with someone. Please do not disturb me."

Zeke and Miles followed him to his shut door, looked at each other, and shrugged their shoulders. This was about the sixth or seventh time he had done this now, ever since Zeke gave him a phone to use. George thought of how much this tool for communication could have helped in his prior life. There was nothing else for Zeke or Miles to do. It was up to President George Washington to pull it together.

As Washington sat in his dressing room, his mind was flooded with the moments in his life where he knew decisive action needed to be taken.

And in all those instances he knew that Providence had selected him to take on that burden. His battles as an officer for the English against the French and Indians, the meeting with the Continental Congress, joining the rabble in Cambridge, Massachusetts, in 1775 to create a Continental Army—these and other trials had given him an overwhelming feeling of obligation and service to other men.

Now, in this "new" body, he could see without much help from Miles the trouble the country was in and was heading for if someone didn't right the sails on the ship of state and head back to the way the country is supposed to function. Government should not control the means of production.

Government should not decide for the people who and what they are. Yes, defense and social order were the Federal Government's roles and to help those who could not or would not help themselves.

He needed to act.

He was being called upon again. And yet he was so weary. "Hello, Jim," Washington said on the phone, "I have some more questions for you. Please come to my dressing room." Jim arrived ten minutes later and slipped into Washington's room.

The convention was starting at 8p.m. sharp. Peters, Miles, and Zeke waited outside of Washington's room. Finally, at 7:50 the door opened. Washington, with his military bearing, struck awe in the three men. How can one-man command so much respect and honor without speaking a word? His physical bearing, even at sixty-five, impressed the three men.

"Shall we depart to the stage, gentlemen?" Washington said as he brushed past them.

"George, how do you want to be introduced?" Peters asked.

"Simply as George Washington, a private citizen who would like to share his ideas with his fellow citizens. I know my name will cause confusion, so you may say I am a descendant of the Washington family."

Peters walked out to the stage where the large and boisterous assembled crowd roared their approval. They knew Peters and Jim Robinson. While Jim had been working in the trenches for the past five years, setting up the party and organizing each state, Malcolm Peters in the last year would accompany him, so now he was also well known and well liked.

"Ladies and Gentlemen," Peters started, "This is a historic meeting. We are here to embark on establishing a new political party. One that best mirrors the will of the people of this county and formed to better all of its citizens. We believe in responsible capitalism. We know that unrestrained capitalism can be harmful, even destructive to societies.

"But with the proper guidelines and government oversight it can function to lift all people's situation in our society.

"We have a guest speaker tonight with a famous name. George Washington is a descendant of the Washington family in Virginia. A private citizen until now, where we have invited him to speak about us, our country, and the future of the Independent Party of America."

There were a few snickers when Washington's name was mentioned, and then it turned into a rousing applause by the audience. Washington walked out onto the stage.

A warm friendly smile was across his face. He wore a blue suit and red tie with a sparkling white shirt. As the applause died down, an audible buzzing began among the people. Something about this man was familiar and powerful to everyone. They just did not know why. The way he held himself, the way he looked at the crowd—something special was happening. You could feel the electricity in the air.

"Thank you all for greeting me so warmly. I have been asked to make a few comments about why we are here tonight. I must tell you from the start I am not one who ever likes any political parties. (Loud applause and laughter.) The reason being that by their nature they become too self-serving, and when that happens, they are more interested in getting and maintaining power than they are in serving the needs of the people. (Applause.)

"So, as I speak to you this evening I must emphasize if we are to be for the people, we must never let politics get in the way of doing what is right for all Americans. (Applause.)

"If we can keep that vision in mind and elect people who talk and act upon only doing the people's will and not their own ambition then there is hope for a new party and perhaps the need for only one party, the Independent Party of America. (Loud applause.)

"What must we do you may ask? What we must do now is not allow this administration's new proposals become law. And we must remove from office those who think a socialist agenda is in the people's best interest. (Applause.) Are you with me? (Thunderous applause.)

"Tonight, we are formally announcing the Independent Party of America. (loud cheering) We are dedicated to the principles that my ancestors wanted for all of us. (Applause.) But a new party needs a backbone. We need to be like our minutemen and be ready to answer the call of our country. (Applause.) So, as my ancestor did 230 years ago, ask yourself will you join me?

"Will you fight for the country we all love?

"Will all rise and cheer the dawning of a new day for our country? (The crowd jumps up, screaming their approval.

Washington is magnetic.) Tonight, we declare that this November a new dawning is coming for our country. It is a new dawning that our founding fathers wanted for us."

Washington stopped and stood from behind the podium. The crowd could hardly contain itself as this imposing man gazed down at all of them. It was as if he was on the balcony in New York over 230 years ago, and the people were welcoming their first president. Suddenly his earpiece came alive.

"Every single senator and representative in Congress who said they would join us has texted us during your speech. They want you to tell the people of their support," Peters said. "I am now going to read some names to you. (The teleprompter came alive with the list of Senators. A screen behind Washington listed all of the new party members from the House of Representatives.)

"You are the backbone of this party. But these are the arms that will fight for us. These are the names of 270 congressmen and women and 52 senators who are leaving their current party and joining the IPA as of this moment." (Wild, frenzied applause.) He proceeded to list the Senators names as the crowd erupted over each name. He kept listing the names through their cheers.

Finally, he stopped. He raised his hands to ask for quiet. Not a sound could be heard among the assembled fourteen thousand.

"We have just saved our country," he said softly, almost inaudible. And then raising his voice, "And now I offer to you the new leader of the IPA, Jim Robinson, whom I nominate as the next President of the United States of America!" Washington greeted Jim and shook his hand and uncharacteristically hugged him.

George waved and left the stage. By the time Jim had finished his rousing speech, American history had been changed.

**CHAPTER 15**

# Who Is that Masked Man?

The media was in a frenzy, as was the current administration.

Washington's speech was played in its entirety to the listing of names by every network in the country. It went viral on the internet with over one billion views. Overnight the current president saw his party's power all but disappear. And so did the Republicans and Democratic parties.

The Congress was in disarray, with a Speaker of the House who no longer was in the majority. Never before did parties get such mass defection while the Congress was in session. Immediately talks started in the White House on how to address this new Independent Party of America.

Many of the senators and representatives who had defected came out with coordinated statements to assure the country that the new political party adhered to the principles articulated at the rally in Charlestown. The planks of the party were laid out and recorded fully for all to read. The outline of the new party's platform was published across the nation. They were presented by the star to emerge from this rally, who was none other than Jim Robinson.

After five painstaking years of making sure that every state had an IPA legally established in the state and then meeting for hundreds of hours with members of Congress to go over in detail the party's platform, he was now the acknowledged head of the party.

They were pleasantly surprised by Washington's endorsement. Jim's stirring speech, after Washington finished, articulated what the new party was going to stand for. He stressed these points above all others:

1. Capitalism would remain the predominant economic system in America. It would not be unrestrained or unregulated capitalism but one that works for all levels of income within our society.

2. This new Capitalism would have a social consciousness. There would be a wealth tax on persons earning above ten million dollars a year. This tax would be used to fund reparations to African Americans and American Indians. These reparations would take the form of free tuition to all charter schools, and State Colleges. The richest in our country would educate the next generation of minority Americans.

3. Institutional racism had to be addressed, admonished and eliminated.

4. The Federal Government's highest priority will be to keep Americans safe. We would maintain our military strength. We would not become embroiled militarily in countries that did not have a direct effect on the wellbeing of our country.

5. States' Rights would be supported by this party.

6.      A new immigration system and policies will be implemented making access to the American way of life from around the world a possibility.

7.      New state schools would be financed with federal funds to create a plethora of trade schools across the country to address the lack of skilled tradesmen in the country.

8.      A planned reduction of the debt to be no more than 2 percent of GDP in twenty years will become an amendment to the constitution (with the exception of a national emergency).

9.      The private/public sector will build one million homes over the next five years for the poor and lower middle-class Americans. The prices of these homes will be government controlled so that they can be afforded by these people in areas like San Francisco and New York.

10.     A measured approach and a plan put in place to address Global Warming. One which required all nations to address their carbon emission equally.

11.     All health care insurance companies will have access to every state. This competition would reduce coverage costs to the level of affordability for all citizens while protecting coverage for pre-existing conditions.

Jim outlined these and other planks of the party and their popularity became apparent across all demographics of our country. He was the superstar and party leader. The media was fixated on all this, but also on the question,

"Who was that masked man?" He looked a lot like George Washington, they agreed, except for the smile, which no one had seen in pictures of the father of our country. But during the rally, Miles and Zeke got George out of town in the RV. George had asked if they could make a trip to Mount Vernon. He wanted to visit home.

All the networks and social media was abuzz with pictures of Washington from the rally. People were measuring facial features compared to historical paintings.

He fit them perfectly along with his height, color of eyes, and size of hands. Now everyone wanted to talk with him, even though the country was in a political turmoil at the moment. No one had seen him come into town or leave town. No hotel records could be found.

A search on the internet found the barest of information and his lineage, but it was there. He apparently was the 14th generation of his family, a distant cousin to Augustus Washington. Someone had taken care of that.

The absence of a more complete background record just got the fires burning brighter to find this guy.

Miles and Zeke watched this phenomenon unfold on their computers and on the TV. George was lost in his own thoughts. No one knew he was going to call out Jim Robinson, but George had been asked weeks ago on his phone by someone, who identified himself only as a friend of Zeke's, to talk to Jim about this possibility.

George took this responsibility seriously and spent literally a hundred hours talking on the phone to Jim about his views on life, government and governing. When he had his first face to face meeting and last conversation with Jim the night of the convention, Washington knew he was the man for this effort. It was during that first and only meeting that he saw that Jim was an African American.

"This" Washington thought as he shook Jim's hand, "is Providence's Hand working. He has given me a chance for redemption in His Eyes."

Now he felt he knew why he had been brought back to this earth. The first thing George did was ask Jim for his forgiveness. Jim had no idea what he was talking about. George told him forgiveness for his family's activities 200 years ago with slaves.

He told Jim it was his families biggest failing to not do more to end this horrible scourge on America. Jim was magnanimous and accepted his heartfelt apology, then they got down to business. Making James F. Robinson the next president of the United States.

After George presented his remarks, he was not buoyed by the response. Everything had been so trying on him since he came into this world. He intellectually understood what in general had happened to him. He understood the amazing scientific advances that had taken place. He understood the political role he just played. He felt from all he read it was necessary. But emotionally and physically he was exhausted. Not only from these activities, but from the fact that this copy was in the middle of HIS presidency.

In spite of holding on to the thought that Providence had led him here and in smally way he hoped he made something right that was so wrong in his life, he was sixty-three years old. He was in the last year of his Presidency. Even then, he had longed to go home with Martha and be a farmer. He served as he knew he had to, but he wanted his private life back.

Those feelings were carried forward in his DNA when Zeke created this copy. So that yearning for home continued to be a predominant thought. He did not want to lead the IPA.

As far as he was concerned, this evening's rally was his first and last appearance. If he could just disappear, he would. He fought for and loved his original life. He did not feel the same way about this one.

"George, we should be getting to Mount Vernon about sunset today." Miles said, "It should still be open to the public. I have a pair of sunglasses and a hat that I would suggest that you wear. Many tourists who are there are deeply fascinated with your life and they would easily recognize you. So, if you don't mind, I'd suggest these."

Miles handed George the items and he went over to the mirror to try them on. He looked like a sophisticated, but cool professor. If it was enough to keep him anonymous that was fine.

They pulled into the parking lot of Mount Vernon at about 3:30 that afternoon. On the way into the estate, George noticed that much of his land had been developed. Houses and paved streets went this way and that. But as they approached the main house, it was as he knew it to be. It remained large and majestic atop a small rise in his property.

A tear rolled down his cheek to see it. Maybe visiting would be too much, but he wanted to see his beloved home.

After they parked the RV, George got out by himself and headed towards the house. He passed the few families with children who could afford to be touring chattering about what they saw. The children were especially excited to see where George Washington lived.

George took in all these impressions. Suddenly, he felt happy and proud that his efforts lived on, touching the lives of everyday Americans this way.

To his side he saw a family from India. The father was talking to his family of about twelve people. He said, "And this man, George Washington, showed the world that we could be free from monarchies. He did not wish to be a king himself or serve a king. He just wanted the United States of America to be the greatest place for people to live in the world. Mahatma Gandhi told his followers that if America could be free of Great Britain, so could India. And his example gave us strength to finally, eventually, gain freedom from England."

As George approached the house, he was asked to buy a ticket for admission, which Zeke, following close behind, took care of.

George strode into his home, well, like he owned it. He removed his glasses and hat and looked around. Some of the rooms were roped off. He understood why, but he still wanted to see his office, where he spent so much time writing letters.

Zeke and Miles distracted the guard, and George slipped into his study. He walked over to his desk and sat down, scanning the desk for the papers that he would have been scattered about. It was sterile and museum-like, not home-like, as he remembered it.

"I am sorry sir, but I'll have to ask you to leave this room." It was Ms. Zola, the curator that Miles and Zeke had met not too long ago.

She then stopped in her tracks. As George looked up at her, she saw *him*. A highly educated woman, steeped in American History, she froze.

"I am sorry. I was just looking around my, or excuse me, President Washington's office." George rose and started for the door. The curator still could not speak. It was as if she was seeing a ghost, but more than a ghost. George departed the room and went outside. She followed him. He went to where a guard was standing next to George and Martha's above-ground crypts, telling the story of the Washington's to visitors.

George bowed his head and sighed deeply, with his hat and glasses in his hand. The curator cautiously approached him.

"You are not the first person to be overwhelmed by this experience," she said. "Many have as much affection for George Washington today, over 230 years since his passing, as in his day. But I must say you have such a remarkable resemblance to him."

George composed himself, "Please pardon me, young lady. I am filled with emotions being here. I am a direct descendant of the family, so I do have a resemblance."

"Are you the man who made that presentation in Charleston last night?"

"Yes, that was me. Were you there?" he asked, not grasping the concept of TV or the internet.

"No, I was not there, but yes, I did see you speak. I keep my politics to myself. But I have to say I was impressed. Your words brought tears to my eyes. You have given me so much hope in this new party.

"And Jim Robinson is so . . . perfect." George turned to leave the grave area and head to the RV. Miles and Zeke waved to Ms. Zola and followed him to the vehicle. George got into the bus and immediately went to the back bedroom and shut the door.

As they started to pull away, Ms. Zola headed for her office and then suddenly stopped in her tracks. The two men, Zeke and Miles, had wanted DNA, and now they are hanging with a guy who looks exactly like George Washington. No, that's crazy, she thought. Couldn't be. Could it? No impossible. She continued to her office, stopped and turned toward the RV and thought, "Did I just see the real George Washington?"

As Miles started up the bus he said to Zeke, "I'm not sure this was a good idea. Who wants to stand over their own grave and peer into their eternal resting place? We cannot put him through anymore of this IPA stuff."

Jim and Peters can take it from here. George teed it up for them, now it's up to them to bring it home. As old as George looks, he looks ten years older after all of this."

"My whole idea of bringing George here was for him to help lead the country in the right direction again. He has. Now let's get him somewhere safe," Zeke said, as he laid down on the couch.

Miles navigated their big rolling home onto the highway heading to Washington, D.C., but instead he went north and then west through Pennsylvania and into Ohio, before he found a campground to part the RV.

"Let's just cook up a meal and eat here, Miles," Zeke said as he bent over, looking into the refrigerator.

That cooling contraption still amazed George. As he joined the others, George pulled himself to his full height to make a statement.

"Thank you for taking me to my home," he said. "It was hard to see the place that I loved the most and not be part of it anymore. Seeing Martha's and my resting place was a disconcerting experience. At times I feel like I am floating in air, attached to nothing. But I must not be remorseful. The good Lord has me here for a purpose, and I must accept His Judgement."

"I have talked to Peters and Jim," Zeke said. "He and Jim feel that what you did has started a peaceful revolution within our country. The new party is launched, espousing the beliefs that you had in founding this country. They feel the sails have been set for this country's re-birth. At this point they do not think they will have to call upon you to further this party's efforts."

"And Jim will lead the party and run for President?" Washington asked.

"Malcolm Peters will be the campaign manager for Jim, Mr. President. Robinson will be the party's nominee for President. He has established his credentials and been groomed for the post these past five years. He will lead the party. The election will be in eight months," said Zeke.

After a pause, he asked a question he'd been wondering about. "How long had you been talking to Jim?"

Washington turned from the refrigerator. "Oh, for many weeks. I received a telephone call on the contraption you gave me.

"It was a man who said he wanted me to call Jim and talk to him. He asked me to vet him for the job. I have not heard that word vet before, but I knew what he meant me to do. He told me that no one better than I could determine if Jim had the right makings to become President.

"The man on the phone did not identify himself, but he said that we might meet some day. I called Jim, and we talked for many hours, on many subjects. He was most impressive. I think he is brilliant. We met before the convention and I knew, just knew he was the right person. I have no doubt he will be a consequential President."

"Did you know Jim is African American?" Washington's face broke into the biggest smile Zeke and Miles had seen this very formal man have since they "met" him. "I am pleased that you have not asked me to play any more part in this process," he said, deflecting the question. "I have for so long wanted to bow out of public life. As I recall, I was in the midst of what I knew would be my last year as President when you terminated my memory. I know they all wanted me to continue another four years. In truth I just wanted to get back to my farm. I was becoming quite weary. Thank goodness, I am done. But what now?"

Miles took out a newspaper he had picked up on the trip. The front-page headline read, "Washington Reappears at IPA's First Convention." The story went on to say that computer analysts had completed computations of this new Washington, and he is exactly the same size and dimensions of Washington in the historical records.

Suddenly there was a knock at the RV door. Zeke looked outside and saw a swarm of fifty newscasters outside the camper. How had the reporters found them?

"Holy smokes, what now, Zeke?" Miles asked. "You know, these reporters won't go away, but what do we do?"

"I'm starting up the RV, and I'm going to carefully get out of here," Zeke said as he hopped into the driver's seat. Then he stopped. There were too many of them. He would end up running over one of them.

Just then a stretch limo drove up to the crowd. Jim Robinson jumped out of the backseat and greeted the crowd of reporters. Jim had been tracking the RV with a device he gave Zeke. He thought Washington might need some cover.

The reporters quickly shifted their attention to Jim and shouted out questions to the dynamic new Presidential candidate. Jim walked away from the RV and stood on a picnic table. He gave a look at Zeke with a quick movement of his eyes, to get out while you can.

"George Washington is a private citizen who agreed to consult for us. He has set the IPA's sails. He is not in good health and is now going back to private life. He is not up to answering any questions. We ask you to respect his request for privacy. I am here, however, to talk about my candidacy," Jim announced.

"We have donations from over a hundred-thousand people who have contributed to our party in the past twenty-four hours. While all of you were focused on other issues these last few years, we have built a grassroots coalition that will take the White House and the Congress this fall. Now, I will take some questions."

"Who is this guy, Mr. Robertson? We have no mention of him until now. Was it just a stunt to find someone looking like George Washington to kick off your convention?"

"No, gentlemen. Mr. Washington is a descendant of Augustus Washington's family tree, George Washington's brother. Thus, the similarity. He is a well-respected man of the community who has contributed greatly to the planks of our party's platform. The party would be nothing without him. But he is a private man who will go back to private life and not partake in any further political issues, events, or discussions.

"He was what we call a behind-the-scenes man. But now his role is over. I would like you to meet with Mr. Peters now to discuss our campaign strategy and where we will be holding our next rally."

With that Malcolm jumped out of the back seat of the car and greeted the reporters. The question-and-answer session would last for over an hour. It drew the people away from the RV, so Zeke gently pulled away from the camp area and headed out the front entrance.

Most of the reporters let them go with barely a glance over their shoulders. Only a couple of cars trailed behind them. Zeke decided he would just out-drive them, and eventually they would go away.

At least he hoped that strategy would work.

They drove for the next six hours on I-70 until they arrived in Finland, Ohio. The reporters gave up after an hour or so and peeled off. The three passengers breathed a sigh of relief, to avoid any questions, at least for now.

They pulled into a Walmart, and George got out. He said he was going shopping

As he walked towards the store, the doors automatically opened. He stood there taking in the ingenuity of such an invention. He wandered towards the back of the store, drawn by a bank of a dozen or more TVs, some up to 80 inches in size. George watched for a few minutes—sports, news shows, cooking shows. He was becoming familiar with the culture; in that they did not puzzle him as much as they had. Amazing technology he thought, but emptier than real life. He then continued on, looking up at the ceiling. The steel struts, piping, and corrugated roof fascinated the builder in him. He walked into the men's clothes section and perused some of the shirts and pants for sale. The price of fifteen dollars for some pants was more than he expected. That amount could be a half-year's salary for his times. Refrigeration still was his favorite thing to see.

He wandered into the deli area and looked at all the meats kept fresh by this method. He studied the array of food on the shelves, the myriad of choices. American's lived better than the kings of Europe, he was sure of it.

After an hour or so of wandering around, George got back out to the camper.

Miles greeted him at the door with news. "I just got a call from Zeke's benefactor. He says we are to turn north and head to this section of Ohio." Miles pointed to a map. "I know it well. It is where my parents lived. They are now passed."

"That is in part of the Ohio Valley, I think, that I surveyed as a young man," George said. "Well, we were asked to get there as soon as possible. So, if we head out tonight and go about five more hours, and then start up again in the morning, we could be there by noon the next day," Zeke said.

"Let's head out then," said George, who was unshaven and looking more casual than usual.

"And I am going to grow a full beard and mustache. That should give me privacy." He was in a particularly good mood. The pressure had been relieved from him, and now he was thinking about what to do next with his new life. He actually started to embrace it as a gift. He decided to shed any further morose feelings. He had read how he had died in 1799, partly from the bleeding that he insisted his physicians do for him. While germs and infections were still a new concept to him, he had learned to embrace the modern science that was presented to him and to understand how the world had moved forward, with knowledge always evolving.

He now saw this progress as not a burden but an adventure to be grateful for and cherished. Yes, he missed Martha, his friends, and family. But he hoped to make new friends, a new life. He was happy. Perhaps as happy as he had been in both lives.

Miles and Zeke took turns and traveled through the night, not stopping as they had planned. In the morning, the GPS settings that Miles had entered brought them to the address given to them by Jim Robinson. It led onto a dirt road.

There was an elaborate fence around the property as far as one could see.

Miles knew the grounds well. It was formerly his parents' farm that he had sold about five years ago. The grounds were beautifully manicured. As they entered the driveway George walked to the front of the RV and sat in the passenger's seat.

"What a beautiful estate," George marveled, as they slowly went up the drive. Trees lined the driveway for about a mile. As it was early spring, they were in full flowery bloom.

On one side a cluster of horses grazed in a pasture—beautiful animals whose form reflected their high pedigree. On the left side of the drive were fields that were neatly laid out and planted with wheat for as far as the eye could see. There must be hundreds of acres with this farm, George thought. Slowly as they went up the drive. Zeke suddenly stopped the RV. He could not believe what he was seeing.

"Hey Miles, what do you see?"

Miles ran up to the front and said, "Holy shit. What the hell?"

Washington was squinting with his mouth agape.

Washington got up and stepped outside. In front of him the driveway had a slight rise. At the top of the rise sat an exact replica of Mount Vernon. Trees and other plantings had been placed around the estate to exactly reproduce the layout that George had planned for his new home when he bought it back in 1758.

He stood staring at the estate. Zeke and Miles sat and watched this great man walk up the slight grade to this beautiful home.

George simply could not believe his eyes. It was as if he were back at Mount Vernon in 1795. Men were working in the fields, planting crops with enormous farm equipment. The barns were bustling with activity. Hog Island sheep were grazing by the hundreds behind the barn.

These were the cash crops that Washington was raising on his farm when he died in 1799. This was just like he never left

Mount Vernon.  Standing in the door of Mount Vernon was a man in his late eighties.

George recognized him from pictures he had seen of him. He was not hard to recognize, with his distinctive hair style. It was Donald Trump.

Zeke and Miles, walking behind George, joined them at the threshold of the estate.

"Welcome my friend, welcome home," Trump said to George, reaching out with his hand to greet the President.

"You have an amazing home, Mr. Trump." George said.

"Oh, this is not my style. This is your home as a gift from the American people to you. We have been working on this home around the clock for several months now. It is almost finished. May I be the first to welcome you home? You have served our country so well. I almost did as good as you did, but you were better, so I wanted this place to be a gift to you. You have over five thousand acres here of private land for you to live on and farm. And no one will bother you out here. I've made sure of that."

"I am awestruck by this, Mr. Trump. I was so happy this morning having finished my efforts for the IPA and looking forward to the rest of my life. This gift fills my heart with tremendous joy."

"You always wanted to retire to your home, I know, and you only had a short time before you got sick. It is only right that some two hundred years later, you get your wish. I know the route here has been a bit unconventional, to say the least. But you have saved the country again, and the least the country can do is give you this life to enjoy for as long as you have.

"Your neighbors, fellow farmers, have arranged a gathering tonight at your home. They want to meet with you if you don't mind." Zeke and Miles joined them at the house front door.

"And Zeke, I've talked to the new CEO of Waltham Scientific Bioworks, and you have your old job back, if that is what you want. It is a new start for you, picking up where you left off, so to speak. Just don't go down the road you went down before, agreed? We have all had enough of that stuff."

"Wendy has asked if you would find some time for her too," Trump continued. "She'd like to make you a nice perfect Manhattan. Miles, I guess you are back to Harvard. You can try and put this all in perspective and be proud of the role you played."

"Thank you, Mr. Trump," Zeke said. "In my memory, Waltham Scientific Bioworks is where I do work. All of these other events have been a diversion or a digression from where I remember I left off. I would love to get back to what I was doing there. Since I cannot remember being fired, it is all good. I feel a little like I'm in the final scene of the *Wizard of Oz*, and the scarecrow, the lion, and the tin man are all getting what they most wanted and most needed, from the Wizard."

"Well, I've never thought of myself that way, but I like it. And Dorothy (pointing at George) gets to go home too! The Great and Wonderful Oz. I think I'll put that on my plane," Trump said, and they all had a good laugh. Except George. He had no idea what they were talking about.

"Don't worry George, I'll get you the movie. Let's go inside, look around the place and meet in your office, George. I want to talk a little politics. And a beard and mustache George, I like that. I like that a lot."

# CHAPTER 16

# He's Baaaaack!!

Later that evening, George's neighbors came by to get acquainted and for some congenial talking and comparing of notes on matters of farming. After they left, George sat and let the events of the day sink in.

He was extremely happy with his new home and the friends he made that evening. The neighbors were excited to meet a descendant from the Washington family and the man who made the speech to save America from itself.

Zeke and Miles came down from the guest rooms in the house to met with George the next morning. "Are you going to be okay?", Zeke asked.

"I am sure I will be fine. I have what I need here to finish my life. Thank you for being good friends to me. I hope we will meet again." George said as he shook their hands good-bye.

"I'd like to come back and talk to you in more detail about your thoughts during the revolution and the subsequent years if you have no objection. I teach history and I would like to get it right." Miles said with a little chuckle.

"Please do come back Miles, but I may not share all my secrets. You know how hard I worked at maintaining the right way to conduct oneself as a President."

Zeke and Miles finally departed and left for a flight back to Logan Airport in Boston and to pick up with their lives and continue what the work they had been doing. The RV was sent back with a private driver provided by Trump.

On his private jet back to Florida, Trump thought about what had transpired over the last eleven or twelve years. When the CEO of Waltham Scientific had called him, after his presidency ended, the executive told him he had a young scientist who had an interesting idea that he might like to get involved in.

He gave him an overview of Zeke's research goal at the time and how he thought it could be safe and good for the world. Trump liked it. Little did he know where it would lead and how it would end up helping the country.

He was sure that Jim Robinson would win the Presidency in the fall. With all the congressmen and senators that defected to the IPA party, legislative progress could be made quickly, and that would straighten the country out in short order. There was just one thing missing.

"Hello, Martha, how are things going?" Trump asked on the phone from his plane. "Did Zeke's old lab equipment function properly?"

"We have just finished our last run, sir. It is just as you instructed. The man's fertilized embryo used DNA from Clint Eastwood's physical characteristics which we spliced with the cognitive aspects of your DNA. It is you at fifty years old, looking pretty much like good old Clint. My, he is so handsome. We have established his name as Mr. Tom Sherwood. His backstory is all in place, all the way to his birth in Brooklyn, New York. There are a bunch of people who remember him well. All clones who love Mr. Sherwood and can be used to verify his existence in the neighborhood, school, and beyond, if needed. He will be a strong running mate for Jim Robinson, and I suspect an excellent President after Jim finishes his terms.

We are now destroying the lab per your instructions. It will never be used again"

"Thank you, Martha. You have been loyal and faithful to me over these many years, in all you have done. And are you sure you are okay coming to work for George in Ohio? I have found a beautiful house for you nearby. I think George would like another Martha in his life, even as an executive secretary."

"Oh, yes, thank you. This plan is exactly right for me. I am looking forward to the change, and I will keep my place in New Hampshire to visit, for vacations. I have had the chair from Zeke's lab sent to me. I will have the listening equipment removed from it once I have it here and treasure it as a keepsake of our important project together."

"I cannot wait to get home to meet *me*," Trump said enthusiastically. "And then get another chance to Make America Great . . . Again.

"Oh, and Martha? Call my hanger in West Palm and tell them I need another name painted on my plane. "The Great and Wonderful Oz."